The
Black
Galaxy

Cast of Characters

ROD CANTRELL
Inventor of the space-drive unit and involuntary captain of the **Stellaris**.

KIT BOWEN
Rod's fiancee and helpmate.

JOE
An expert electrician, trapped like Rod and Kit aboard the **Stellaris**.

COLONY LEADER
Member of an alien species whose survivors are found by Rod.

Also — other artisans and girl biologists trapped on **Stellaris,** bulbuous headed pyramid-people with attentuated limbs and the little, round folk of the planet of the dead cities.

The Black Galaxy

By *MURRAY LEINSTER*

GALAXY SCIENCE FICTION NOVEL No. 20

Galaxy Publishing Corp.   421 Hudson St., New York 14, N. Y.

GALAXY *Science Fiction* Novels, selected by the editors of
GALAXY *Science Fiction* Magazine, are the choice of science
fiction novels both original and reprint.

GALAXY *Science Fiction* Novel No. 20
35c a copy. Subscription: Six Novels $2.00

PRINTED IN THE UNITED STATES OF AMERICA
by
THE GUINN COMPANY, INC.
NEW YORK 14, N. Y.

CHAPTER ONE

Grounded!

HE Chairman of the Space Project Committee was very
polite. But he was a politician and Rod Cantrell had been
a soldier and was a very famous man and all politicians
know that soldiers and other practical men can be most obsti-
nate when politics shows clearly what should be done.

"Permit me to congratulate you," the Chairman said blandly,
"on your promotion."

"On being kicked upstairs?" asked Rod drily. "I'm not pleased.
It looks to me—since that's what I came to protest about—that
I'm promoted to something like a dummy job so that the work
I want to do and the decisions I need to make will be made
by people who think more of elections than of really impor-
tant things."

The Chairman of the Space Committee laughed apprecia-
tively. But he made a mental black mark. This man would not
be amenable to political pressure. Perhaps he had better be a
little more thoroughly deprived of authority—and given more
prestige to make up for it.

"Oh, come, come!" he said indulgently. "What have you to
complain of? The ship you're building has certainly all the funds
anyone could need!"

"I think," Rod said flatly, "that we should postpone any at-
tempt at interplanetary travel until we get some interplanetary
weapons." As the Chairman beamed at him he went on doggedly.

"I designed the drive-units for the ship we're building, for the
one now under construction. I made the first interplanetary
flights—the only ones made to date. But I urge the postpone-
ment of exploration until we have some defense. The weapons
we have now would be useless against an enemy with space-
ships."

5

The Chairman beamed on and offered Rod a cigar. Rod curtly refused it.

"Yet," mused the Chairman amiably, "you did not encounter any other space-ships in your three interplanetary flights, you cannot name possible enemies and you have not any real evidence that this—ah—hypothetical enemy you speak of has weapons superior to our own. After all, we have a gift for destruction ourselves! And remember, the idea of space-conquest has caught the imagination of the public!"

Rod set his jaws. He was prepared to be made ridiculous if he could bring about some measure of defense against the dangers he foresaw. But a politician could not be expected to believe anything dangerous if it brought in votes. And the proven possibility of travel, not only to other planets but to the stars, had roused enormous popular enthusiasm.

"There were Martians, once," said Rod. "There aren't anymore. They had a civilization that in some ways was higher than ours. You've seen the proofs of that. And they were wiped out. They simply vanished leaving their cities to fall in ruins behind them."

"You assume that your—ah—hypothetical space-travellers destroyed them?"

"I do," said Rod. He added with some irony, "You must remember that I saw the dead Martian cities with the least stray possession left in place and what I believe were the remains of the Martians lying where they dropped. And I saw that pyramid on Calypso, which surely no men made. It was made by the race I'm talking about, which I haven't seen, which I can't name or describe, but which made it to lure the first man to see it into sending them a signal that space-travel had been achieved on Earth."

"Yet you did not even photograph it," said the Chairman, tolerantly. "And you insist that we devote research and money to weapons—when the world is very weary of weapons and of

War—instead of upon space-travel, which has filled humanity with optimism it has never known before! My dear sir, it would be political suicide!"

"The point is," said Rod bitterly, "that not to do it may be physical suicide!"

"Now, now." The Chairman beamed cordially. "I shall confer with the rest of the Committee. You have just had a promotion and perhaps we can manage another. We are fully aware of your services in the past and you are surely the only interplanetary voyager, so you cannot be contradicted. But you ask the making of a very unpopular decision! Suppose we raise you another step in rank?"

Rod stood up, rather pale.

"I'm not trying blackmail," he said bitterly. "I'm trying to drive some sense into your head! There are more important things than winning elections, and staying alive is one of them! I can resign my commission and speak publicly of what I fear."

The Chairman's smile remained, though he spoke acidly.

"I am afraid the popular impression would be that you wish to prevent further space-voyages, to keep the credit of being the only man who had ever crossed space. I am sure that—ah—other officers who are your equals in rank would look at it that way. I shall discuss the matter with my Committee. Meanwhile you are, of course, under regulation obligations not to make public statements without official clearance. We will see about another promotion for you."

He bowed Rod out, beaming at him benevolently. And Rod was sick with apprehension. He'd wanted to have the first real spaceship capable of putting up a fight. He believed it might need to fight. But anyhow he was still in command of the construction of the space-ship now building and he'd command it when it took off from Earth.

Maybe he could find more conclusive proof of the peril he

believed in. Most likely, indeed, on the Moon. The central peak of Tycho would be the logical place to look for proof. If he could show a group of scientists that proof. . . . But as it turned out he wasn't to be allowed to do anything so sensible.

Two days later he had his orders. He had a promotion. And all real authority was taken from him. He was again kicked upstairs, to a desk, and he was transferred to another branch of the service. He received the warmest possible thanks for the value of his contributions to the project from which he was now relieved. He went sick all over. And when he told Kit Bowen about it he could have wept with impotent fury. She looked at him indignantly.

"It's not fair!" she cried. "You designed the ship, Rod, and you're the only one who will really know how to run it, anyway, and—and—"

Rod tried to grin at her, but he couldn't. It was too important. Much more important than his own feelings in the matter.

But he said somehow through stiff lips, "I'll show my successor everything I know, Kit. And I'll try to make him believe in what I'm worried about."

Kit stamped her feet. Then she turned away to keep him from seeing that she wanted to cry. But she didn't really understand the gone feeling inside of Rod at that.

They stood beside the hulk of the *Stellaris*, which was just two-thirds completed. The ship was a hundred-odd feet long and forty-some through. It was a space-ship—the first vessel ever built on Earth to navigate the regions between the stars. Rod Cantrell had designed it, after making the first human interplanetary flights in a modified captured weapon taken from the rebels in the war of the Total State against the Earth Government.

He'd seen the possibility of a space-drive in a device that had been created only for mass murder and the drive he'd worked out was no makeshift calling for centuries of develop-

ment before men could aspire to the stars. His first flight in
the toy-sized altered weapon took him to the Moon with absolute ease and safety.

His second was equally safe and precise and it took him to
Mars. He brought back photographs and artifacts for proof.
And the third flight, aimed at a more distant objective to check
the physical constants governing the space-drive, had reached
Calypso, the largest of Jupiter's moons.

That makeshift craft, though, could only make flights as
stunts. The *Stellaris* had been begun to carry an adequate
crew of scientists for the study, first of Sol's other planets,
ultimately for roaming the stars so that human colonies could
begin to spread throughout the Galaxy. Rod Cantrell had been
given charge of the ship's construction, and he had been promised her command.

But now he'd been handed orders from the Space Project
Commission which dashed all his hopes. He was not only relieved of the duty of supervising the *Stellaris'* construction but
was bluntly informed that he would not even be a member
of her crew when she left Earth—because of his wild tale of
an inimical race, possessing space-ships, which would threaten
the peace of Earth.

Kit said, gulping, "It's not fair, Rod! It's stupid! It's unjust!
You deserve—"

"That doesn't matter," said Rod. "What does matter is what
can happen. This decision is on account of my report on that
pyramid on Calypso."

"But you did the right thing!" insisted the girl. "There wasn't
anything else to do!"

"That was my opinion," said Rod, "but the Commission does-
n't agree. I think they feel that I consider myself too famous
and that I'd like to stop space-travel so I'd stay the only man
who ever achieved it."

"Nonsense!" scoffed Kit.

"They've suspected that report from the beginning," Rod added. "They've never allowed any reference to the pyramid to be published. They said it would cause public alarm. Of course, it would imperil their jobs.

"Their places were created to encourage space exploration. If they discouraged it, instead, the Commission will be scrapped and they'll have no salaries. I hate to think of so great a risk being run just so some political appointees can stay on salary."

Kit Bowen made a scornful sound. She wasn't exactly engaged to Rod, because engagements were no longer considered matters that existed formally to be announced. But they had planned to marry. Rod knew now that it had become doubtful. He could have played it more or less safe, and guided a scientific expedition in the *Stellaris* in search of proof of what he knew.

But he'd tried it the right way, with full reports and an effort to throw the Committee behind research for defense. As a result, he was kicked upstairs. He'd never have another chance. And to be a permanent desk-officer—Kit wouldn't care, but he would.

Riveters pounded on the *Stellaris'* metal skin like monster woodpeckers hunting giant grubs. They were putting on the flotation-bulges, designed to make her float merrily, even if she landed in a sea of liquid ammonia.

The air-lock construction-doors of the ship opened. Electricians came out and headed for the commissary for lunch. Two girls, no doubt assistants in biology working on the air-purifying plant, also came out of the lock, chattering, and went briskly to the same place.

The air-system for the ship was already installed and was being tested by being run to purify the air used by workmen on the inside of the already-sealed hull. The ship's corridors were still bare metal though and it would be many weeks yet before the living quarters were fitted out, the computers and astrogation instruments put in, even the first of the ship's stores accumulated.

But the field-generators and tractor and pressor beams were in and had already been tried out. The ship would positively go anywhere in the galaxy that her crew demanded, though she was the first Earth-ship ever built for space-travel. Only Rod knew that she wasn't the first space-ship. There were others.

The thing was that the crews of the other ships, roaming among the stars, weren't human crews and they wouldn't welcome human competition.

He'd learned that from a silvery-metal pyramid, some thirty feet of seamless stuff on every side. It was out on Calypso, on the very peak of the i.'ghest and most singular of the mountains of that sub-satellite. It had not been built on Calypso and certainly men hadn't made it but the creatures who had made it knew that men existed.

There were bas-reliefs of human forms upon its brightly-gleaming metal sides and there were two human-size metal doors that could obviously be opened by simply turning the handles of two human-sized locks. Its location was one that would certainly be visited by any human explorer of Calypso, if only so that he could leave a record of his visit there for later voyagers to find. And that so-human pyramid, suggesting earlier visitors still, would almost irresistably impel the first man to reach Calypso to turn the door-handles and go in.

But Rod Cantrell hadn't done that. Perhaps because of war experience, perhaps because he didn't like the artwork. He cut into the structure with a thermite torch, leaving the doors alone. He found it packed with machinery which surely wasn't of human design, and he struggled to understand it.

In the end he found a power-storage unit that was far and away beyond anything of human manufacture. He cut the power-leads and traced connections. And then he caused the

doors to open. In opening they swung contacts and controls and
he saw that they'd have sent the power—some hundreds of
millions of kilowatts —in a mighty surge of energy through a
devi̇ he didn't begin to understand but which was obviously
some sort of radiation-generator.

And instantly thereafter the whole pyramid and its machines
began to smoke and were glowing faintly by the time he got
out of it. It melted itself and dissolved in a pool of melted
metal—which exploded when the cut-off power-unit blew. So
that he had nothing but a verbal description to offer with his
report —and he wasn't quite believed.

CHAPTER TWO

Take-Off

NOW he stood beside the incomplete hulk of the *Stellaris*
with the orders that ended his career in his hand.

"It still seems to me that I did the right thing," Rod
said bitterly. "I guessed it as a sort of booby-trap. It was a
gadget to signal somebody, somewhere, when men climbed up
to the point of achieving space-travel! And who'd want to be
warned when we reached that stage? Not friends certainly! If
they'd been friendly they'd have helped!"

"Of course they would!" said Kit with conviction.

"I kept that signal from being sent," said Rod. "If I'd kept
my mouth shut I'd have commanded the *Stellaris* and we'd
have found another one—there's probably another on the central peak in Tycho's crater on the Moon—and I could have
made the Commission see it.

"But I had to tell about it, believing my word would be taken.
So now somebody else will take the *Stellaris* out and it'll be
pretty odd if the signal doesn't get sent off when he finds another

pyramid. And then what'll happen? What would we do if we'd been traveling among the stars for ages and found a new, up-start race getting ready to compete with us? And a rather pugnacious race, at that? We'd smack them down and fast!"

Kit said, agreeing fully, "If we found them before they'd reached that point we'd try to make friends with them."

"Whoever built the pyramid found us," said Rod, drearily. "Maybe a few thousand years ago. Maybe at the time they knocked off the Martians. They didn't bother exterminating us then. We weren't worth the trouble, though the Martians were."

He shrugged his shoulders hopelessly. "Anyhow I've got my orders. Somebody'll come to take over from me within hours. I'm going to take a last look over the ship and then clear my desk and get ready to leave. Want to come with me?"

Wordlessly she pressed his arm. They went together to the air-lock. Rod Cantrell composed his face so that nobody could guess his inner feelings. The lock-doors opened and they entered.

Immediately there was the oddly pleasant smell of growing things which came from the air-purifying set-up. It was partly experimental still, but it demonstrably worked. The air in the ship had been kept fresh and breathable for more than six weeks, despite the men who worked inside the hull, by specially-bred plant life kept in hydroponic tanks.

There were chemical purifiers in reserve of course but nor-mally the ship's air would be restored to normal as the air of Earth is kept sweet—by plants. There was even a section of the air-room in which food-plants were being tried out for the same purpose, turning out foodstuffs as a byproduct of the purification of the ship's atmosphere.

In hydroponic tanks, vegetables grew with amazing luxuri-ance. The *Stellaris* would not be quite self-sustaining but there should be at least occasional meals of dewy-fresh vegetables even when the ship was on the far side of Orion.

Rod Cantrell and Kit stepped into the unfinished interior

of the ship. The smells of work were noticeable, though work had stopped for the lunch-hour. Rod looked lonesomely about. In all probability, he would never set foot in the *Stellaris* again.

The smell of vegetation was strong and pleasant, but there was the smell of paint too and the curious odor of heated metal cooling off—all the aromas of uncompleted construction. In a room designed for storage four painters ate their lunch companionably from lunch-boxes, rather than bother to leave the ship. An electrician smoked restfully beside his tools.

They went into the engine-room, in which there would be no single massively-moving part. A tiny isotopic generator made its humming noise. It was built around a block of artificially radioactive material which gave off electrons alone, with no neutrons or mesons or gamma rays. It yielded utterly safe power and when its total output was not needed for the ship's purposes, the excess free electrons were absorbed in another artificial isotope, which, in absorbing them, become converted into the parent substance.

A fuel-supply for years of operation thus had necessarily been built into the ship when it was made.

The field-generators, too, were all complete. They had been tested with the *Stellaris* safely anchored at bow and stern with tractor-beams. Rod regarded the generators hungrily. He'd designed them and they had features of which he was very proud. But now he'd never be able to see for himself how his designs stood up under service conditions.

"You know how the force-fields work," he said almost wistfully to Kit. "In theory there are an indefinite number of dimensions, therefore an indefinite number of—I suppose you'd call them universes—in parallel. Our universe hangs together because all its parts attract each other magnetically and there are gravitational linkages all through space.

"There's an incredibly complex network of electrostatic stresses by which even island universes attract each other. So our

universe is stable. But if all the forces that link an object to
our cosmos—the things that tie it in—are cut it falls out of the
universe we know.

"It goes apparently into a dark universe, where there seem
to be no stars. Maybe it's a dead universe where the process
of entropy is complete, where all the energy of the system
has run down. But we don't know yet."

Kit nodded wisely. In the late rebellion of the Total State
the city of Pittsburgh had vanished between two heart-beats
with some millions of human beings. Washington had been
slated to go next and Rod Cantrell had been duped—or so it
was thought by the war lords of the Total State—into operating
the weapon which would destroy it.

But he'd understood their weapon a little too well and it had
been turned terribly against them by his understanding. Now
the Earth Government ruled undisputed again—and the Earth
Government had taken from Rod his chance to go with the
Stellaris to the void between the stars. Because he'd made a
report that nobody wanted to believe. . . . .

"These generators," said Rod wistfully, "make a field close
about the Stellaris which cuts every natural link between the
ship and the million-billion suns of our universe. Electrostatic
stresses can't go through that field. Gravitation doesn't penetrate.
Magnetic lines of force are stopped. So the ship leaves our universe. As Pittsburgh did. Only—we leave one link of our own
making.

"We leave a tractor-beam in existence pulling the ship toward
one spot. A tractor-beam can penetrate the field that cuts off
everything else. And the ship is drawn to the one spot the
tractor-beam is focussed on, although it moves in a parallel
universe and isn't in our cosmos at all. When it stops at the object the beam is pulling we cut off the force-fields and apparently
fall back into our own space. But we've traveled!"

Kit nodded again. She knew all this of course but Rod was

heartbroken and it helped him to talk.

"And," he said wistfully as he led the way out of the engine-room, "a pressor-beam works the same way. We can push away from a place we want to start from, instead of waiting for a tractor to reach out a few light-years to our destination."

He sounded almost enthusiastic as he went along the straight-line corridor between the engine-room and the control-cabin—as yet practically empty of controls.

"My trip to Calypso proved," he added, "the mass-inertia ratio in the dark universe I actually traveled in, isn't the same as in our universe. The speed of light is higher—much higher. The time I took to get to Mars suggested it and the trip to Calypso proved that the constants of the two spaces are different. I reached Calypso through the dark universe faster than light could make the trip through ours!"

Then he stopped. He'd reached the control-room from which he'd expected to direct the *Stellaris*. There was the big instrument-board with practically none of the intended instruments set into place. The switches that had been installed were taped to the "off" position, to avoid accident. They'd been used just once, when the force-field generators were tried out and the ship — kept from traveling by anchoring tractor-beams holding her fast—had gone into the dark universe for minutes.

"But," said Rod, after an instant, "that's that."

He stood grimly in the ship he was now forbidden to command.

Then, just as he turned to lead Kit outside again, there came a sudden sharp crackling sound from somewhere in the ship. It had the violent harsh timbre of an electric arc. Somebody shouted frantically. By sheer instinct Rod Cantrell plunged toward the scene of emergency.

But he didn't get there. Suddenly he seemed to be falling endlessly, horribly, nightmarishly, with no weight and no grip on anything. There were vision-ports in the control-room, intended to permit a view of a landscape or of the stars. As the crackling roar grew thunderous those vision-ports turned red, then orange, then flashed through the spectrum to violet and beyond.

The vision-ports became filled with utter blackness and on the instant the control-room was as dark as any cave on Earth and Rod and Kit seemed to be hurtling blindly through sheer opacity. Kit uttered a strangled cry. She had left the floor when weight vanished. She had the hysterical sensation of an increasing, breathtaking dive.

There were screamings somewhere. There was a strange metallic smell of vaporized cable. There was a pungent reek of ozone. The roaring seemed to grow yet louder and the panic-stricken cries grew with it. There came the stench of burned insulation and then of sooty smoke.

Kit cried out again, "Rod!"

He said in a coldly savage voice. "Steady! You're not falling. The fields went on from a short-circuit somewhere in the ship. Now the ship's on fire and we're in the dark universe—traveling. Steady!"

A little flicker of light—flame—appeared in the corridor leading to the engine-room. There was enough light to show Rod, floating helplessly in the air, inches only from a featureless metal wall. Kit drifted yards from any solidity, her eyes wide and filled with fear.

But the light helped. Rod twisted himself and kicked. He went tumbling—head-over-heels away from the wall—to the floor, where he grasped the edge of the incomplete control-panel. He swung himself about. The light flickered again, and he leaped, diving through weightlessness for the corridor.

He went soaring into it and a mushrooming mass of yellow incandescence licked out of it. Kit screamed. But the flame died away a little as he plunged into it, flared out again only when he was almost through, so that it barely singed him. He went plunging on into the engine-room.

Unable to stop, he floated until his out-stretched arms cushioned his impact against the far wall. He swung about again and soared a second time—this time for the humming small isotopic generator which supplied the electric current for all the ship.

He reached it. He held fast—it was extraordinary hard to hold fast with no weight to help—and savagely cranked off the manual switch which had kept the unit inert during shipment. The roaring of the arc died instantly. There was only an ominous booming noise as paint and insulation and construction-stores heated by the arc continued to burn. But even that tended to die down without the arc to keep the flame supplied with vaporized fuel.

Then Rod looked at the ports in the wall of the engine-room, and cold sweat came out all over him. The ship was incomplete. It was unequipped. It had no stores at all. But it had taken off from earth. There were stars in view out the vision-ports, now that the force-field had cut off and the ship was back in normal space. But it wasn't on Earth. It wasn't on any planet.

And there wasn't any sunlight shining in any of the ports. There weren't—this made Rod's throat go dry when he threw himself across the dark vacancy of the engine-room to one port after another and stared out—there weren't even any familiar constellations. The *Stellaris* had had a speed and kinetic energy of its own by virtue of the shared motion of the Earth on its axis and around the sun, and the other motion of the solar system as a whole.

It had gone into the dark universe where the constants of mass and inertia were strange and still unexplored. There was not even a bright yellow star anywhere in the heavens which might be Earth's sun at a greater distance than usual. The *Stellaris* was somewhere among the stars. Earth and its sun could be anywhere, in any direction, at almost any distance up to light-millennia away. There was no possible way to tell. Even worse—

The ship, in fact, was a derelict. It had been designed to be driven by the reaction of its tractor and pressor-beams upon solid bodies outside of itself. Now, apparently, the nearest solid objects were the stars. It would take years for the beams to reach the nearest and there was no instrument on board by which the nearest might even be chosen. There were no stores of food, no star-maps, no trained crew—there was no faintest reasonable ground for hope nor reason for any effort.

But Kit was on board. So when the flames died down and only a penetrating, noisesome reek of burned paint filled the air, Rod Cantrell turned on the isotopic dynamo once more and switched on lights throughout the ship.

Painfully he began the process of searching the unfinished hulk for unwilling members of its company, to calm them and sooth them and threaten them in preparation for labors he had yet to imagine, for purposes he had yet to devise, toward ends he could not even conceive of. Oddly enough, he did not even think of the alien race that had been the cause of his uneasiness back on Earth. But here among the stars was where the greatest danger lay.

CHAPTER THREE

Contact

THAT danger manifested itself within hours. The short-circuit had been repaired—a painter had shifted some welding-rods to make room for a comfortable nap during his lunch-hour, and so had made a contact between two exposed wires from which take-off leads were to have led current elsewhere.

Lights again burned throughout the ship and Rod had turned on all pressor-beams in the rather desperate hope that somewhere within their range there might be some solid substance to give the ship navigability. Actually the most he hoped for was something to drive toward or from so that there could be acceleration and the feel of gravity to hearten the bewildered and frightened people who were the *Stellaris'* unwilling crew.

They were turned on and almost immediately he thought he felt a slight stirring of the ship. It was too slight to be sure. When he held a coin at arm's length and let it go, it stayed there in mid-air. If anything had been touched by the beams it had been lost—had slipped out of them. The nightmarish feeling of perpetual falling continued. Reason did no good. The sensation was nerve-racking.

Then, suddenly, a flash of unbearable light poured in through the vision-ports. It lasted no longer than a flash-bulb's flare, and was gone again. But Rod dived for a port and stared out. Instantly he blinked, blinded. As he reached the glass window opening upon all of space a second flash came.

It was blindingly bright—but it came from a tiny spot, an infinitesimal spot, no larger than a star-image. A pause, then a third flash came. It would make the ship's hull glow as if incandescent. And the third flash was not from the same place as the second.

Rod was dazed for an instant. He had a flash of hope. Then he knew better. He'd had the pressor-beams turned on at random. They'd touched something which had sped on out of the pressor-beam field. Now that something flashed a search-beam. And there was but one possible source for brief unthinkably-bright flashes of light which would last only for thousandths of a second.

Only in space would a light-beam have certain advantages over radar. On Earth radar penetrates clouds and mist. In space there are no hindrances to vision. If there were a space-ship

somewhere off there in the void and if it had detected the
Stellaris' pressor-beams and dived out of them, it might use
radar to locate the Earth-ship.

It would learn more from a single flash of visual light, yielding
a photograph, than any scanning-beam could report in hours.
The fact was wisdom after the event but it told Rod instantly
that there was a space-ship yonder. And no space-ship could
be friendly.

He went into frenzied activity. He dived back to the engine-
room and swung the pressor-beams in tense and urgent quest.
Spreading them wider at first he searched for something for
them to react against. He found it. He felt the ship stir. He put
on more power. The ship surged ahead. More power still and
he felt the floor-plates push against his feet. He put on more
power and more and more . . .

In seconds the Stellaris was thrusting away from something
unseen at a full gravity acceleration. In minutes more it was
a gravity and a half. Rod worked grimly with a small pressor,
hunting for a focus so the beam could be locked to the object
it was to thrust away from.

The acceleration increased. The fan-shaped pressors were
pushing against something which came closer despite the re-
pulsive force of the beams the Stellaris played on it. There was
an arrogant confidence in the other space-ship, which seemed
to be testing out the maximum power the Stellaris could exert. Sweat came out on Rod's forehead.

Then, suddenly, the small pressor found a focus and locked and he struggled feverishly against nearly two gravities
to the control-room. Just as he laid his hands on the force-
field switches there was a sudden sickening loss of all but the
most minute sensation of weight as the other ship darted out
of the pressor-beam and came flashing up beside the unwieldy
Stellaris.

Rod had one glimpse of it as he flung the force-field

switches home. It was pyramidal. It blanked out a triangular patch of stars. Rod felt a momentary deathly giddiness —and then the force-fields closed in. The *Stellaris'* ports went ebony-black and it was again in the dark universe.

Whatever weapon the enemy ship intended to use did not follow into the dark cosmos, but the Earth-ship's focussed pressor did not penetrate its own force-fields and thrust and thrust and thrust—with all the power Rod dared to put into its coils.

The hulk went streaking madly through the utter blackness of its private cosmos for second after second — and nothing happened — and then for minute after minute, then for hour after hour.

For a long time Rod stood grimly at the incomplete instrument board, expecting any instant to feel that deadly giddiness and then death. Some weapon had been used against the *Stellaris* and he felt sick and weak and ill.

But after a long time he went down to the engine-room again and examined the single small pressor-beam he'd focussed and locked on the pyramidal ship and its point of focus was very, very far beyond the point at which it had been set. He could not guess the distance. There had been no chance to calibrate the controls. But it was very, very, very far away indeed.

After twelve hours the pressor could no longer adjust to the increasing distance. The pyramidal ship went beyond its range. The locked focus went off and the ship hurtled blindly on through black emptiness.

"They haven't got our force-fields," Rod told Kit, grimly. "There's that much gained. They couldn't follow us when we vanished. At least we can play hide-and-seek with them!"

Kit had heard from him about the momentary glimpse he'd had of the other craft.

"That feeling we had," she said with a shudder. "I thought

I was dying. So did everybody else."

"We probably were," he said evenly. "If it had lasted a fraction of a second longer they'd have caught the ship. They'd have examined our corpses and they'd probably have reported and had the records searched. They'd know that people of our structure should have set off a gadget on Calypso — only we didn't. I suspect we're not the only lucky people right now!"

An hour later he said abruptly, "I'm going to cut the field. That ship is a long way off. First I'm going to set the pressor-beams at a wide angle as a warning system. But we ought to do something better. . . ."

He hand-set the beams so that the ship would be sur-rounded by a shield of repulsion on every side. Any ship or planet or even meteroite that might be within range when the *Stellaris* returned to normal space would bring about a repulsion of the ship itself.

Having no detection-instruments, they could tell of the near-ness of a solid object they could not see by the stirring of the ship itself. Then he threw the switches again, to let the *Stellaris* drop back into the universe of stars.

A myriad-myriad suns surrounded them, each so remote that it was but a pin-point of light. Again there was no fa-miliar portion of the galaxy within view. There was the Milky Way, to be sure, but even that seemed to have changed its aspect. It was markedly brighter on one side than the other — and Earth is not too far, on a cosmic scale, from the center of the First Galaxy.

The *Stellaris* had fled at uncountable multiples of the speed of light while in the dark universe. It was certainly many thousands of light-years from Earth, with no possible indi-cation either of its first course or of its second in departing from it.

Rod stayed in normal space for four hours, and the pressor-beams told of no solid object within four light-hours' distance. Grimly, he went back to the dark universe. The kinetic energy of the *Stellaris'* acquired velocity remained.

In normal space it meant a certain speed in an unknown direction. In the dark universe that speed was multiplied. He kept the ship in blackness for half an hour, browbeating an electrician meanwhile into beginning the assembly of a short-short-wave receiver.

Out into normal space again — and still no star within view which seemed nearer than any other. He had a course of action planned out, which was almost hopeless but not quite. He went back into the dark universe once more.

Six times within the next twenty-four he came back to normal space. Five times the *Stellaris* was utterly alone in the center of mockingly remote stars.

But the sixth time — and it was only chance — the *Stellaris* winked into being in normal space and there was a giant yellow sun perceptibly nearer. It had at least a visible disk and flaring prominences leaped and curled outward from its sides. More, there were planets. No less than four were plainly visible and a monster world — snow-covered from pole to pole — swam within naked-eye view from the vision-ports. He waited with taut nerves beside the force-field switches.

A bellowing voice came from somewhere below him in the ship. *"No-o-o-o radar!"*

That was the electrician beside his short-short-wave receiver. Only voice signals could be used in the uncompleted ship because there was no intercommunication system in being.

Rod waited. The pressor-beams spread out, out and out at the speed of light. Rod was hollow-eyed and jumpy. There was a stubble of beard on his chin. He had been doing four men's work under heavier responsibility than any man or men should ever be required to accept, because he believed that on the safety or utter destruction of the *Stellaris* hung the safety of the human race. But he had no choice.

The voice came again from below, *"No-o-o-o radar!"*

The *Stellaris* then, was not being scanned. Not yet, any-how. The ship stirred ever so slightly. The pressor-beams, fanning out, had reached the snow-covered planet. Rod called orders and the beams were narrowed.

The repulsion was from that planet only. Unless a space-ship were in exact direct line between the *Stellaris* and the planet there was nothing in space that was menacing. The odds were good. But Rod waited a long half-hour, with the *"No-o-o-o radar!"* at regular intervals, before he even began to relax.

"I guess we're safe for the moment," he said wearily. "We'll have to take a chance anyhow. Kit, we want a tractor put on that planet yonder — not the near one but the next one in toward this sun. We'll time it, of course."

Even then he waited tensely. The invisible, narrowed trac-tor-beam reached out at a hundred-and-eighty-two-thousand miles a second. Four minutes — five — then a perceptible jerk. The planet was in the neighborhood of fifty-five million miles away but now the ship was being drawn toward it.

"Rod," said Kit anxiously, "you're terribly tired! Can't I stand watch for you? It'll be hours and hours before we get there!"

"It'll be days," said Rod wearily. "We'd better stay in nor-mal space for this trip. But I'll fix a gadget. If those pyramid devils can't follow us into the dark universe we can fool them at that."

He surrendered the controls to her. He improvised a spring which would throw on the force-fields and keep them on if the person on watch should be killed by a weapon like that they had experienced.

"Get somebody to hold this," he said tiredly. "There's enough pull to give us the feeling of gravity. And I've got a sort of idea."

CHAPTER FOUR

Dead World

H E SAT down to draw plans and make calculations. But within seconds he was asleep. It was not only the sixty-some hours of unremitting tensity but the strain of worrying about what might be happening back on Earth that had worn him out. It would be believed of course that he had taken off in the *Stellaris* deliberately as an act of resentment at having his command taken away from him.

And of course he would be classed as a traitor or murderer or worse and immediately the Space Project Committee would set to work to duplicate the *Stellaris* and send it off — undoubtedly without orders to be wary of metal pyramids. He had to get back to Earth in time to stop that — which was patently impossible. He could not hope to get the *Stellaris* or Kit back to Earth at all.

He slept and Kit stood valiantly beside the almost empty control-board. The *Stellaris* moved on toward the unnamed planet of an unknown sun, its acceleration giving the effect of weight for its occupants. Word went about the oddly-assorted ship's company of an approaching landing, and they cheered.

The girl biologists, in charge of the air purifying plant, brought it back to proper functioning. The hydroponic vegetables had borne a small crop of edibles, despite the alternations of gravity with no gravity at all. The crop was very small but there were not many to eat it. Four painters, two electricians, three arc-welders and five girls had remained in the ship during the lunch-hour which seemed so long ago.

Presently a painter came to the control-room to present a complaint. Kit put her finger to her lips, pointed to Rod and beckoned. She explained the significance of the spring, whispering, and made Rod as comfortable as she could without

waking him. Then she went about the ship, talking earnestly
to every individual.

It was a very good idea, because with continued normal
feeling of weight, something like normal mental processes
returned to the unwitting voyagers. They began to realize that
none of Earth's other planets was suited for human use and
that it was not likely that this unknown world would be of
any value for them.

They realized, too, the utter lack of preparation for inter-
stellar travel. There was not even food, save for the garden
in the air-purifying room. But Kit managed to change their
forebodings to no worse than anxious curiosity and when they
had reached that stage they were prepared to act as intelli-
gently as they could. So the situation, as far as the crew was
concerned, was much more hopeful.

Kit waked Rod when their chosen planet loomed large before them. He opened his eyes as a voice bellowed monotonously, *"No-o-o radar!"* from somewhere below in the ship.

"We're almost there," said Kit anxiously, "and we don't
know how to land."

Rod was instantly awake. He stared at the disk — big as a
dinner-plate — on the planet ahead. The sensation of weight
proved that the *Stellaris* was hurtling toward it at ever-in-
creasing speed.

"We'll switch to pressor-beams and slow up," he said. "So
far, pretty good!"

He sent calls through the ship, warning of the change-over.
There was a bare second of weightlessness, then all floors became ceilings and all ceilings floors. It was purely a guess-
work process. Rod could estimate the planet's distance only
by the time needed for the pressor-beams to hit it.

He could not estimate the ship's speed at all. But he set
to work to improvise landing tactics by rule of thumb. As a
first measure he shifted the beams to one side of the planet,

so that the *Stellaris* would no longer head straight for the center of the visible hemisphere.

It was necessary to remember that the danger from alien space-ships might easily be greater here than anywhere else in the universe. The *Stellaris* might actually have come back to normal space so far within the empire of the pyramid-builders that radar beams and scouts were considered unnecessary. She could, conceivably, be heading for the very stronghold of the alien race and could have been undetected only because such an approach was unimaginable. But it was not likely.

The Ship's course altered almost imperceptibly. She had been approaching too fast for an endurable stop short of the strange world's surface. Now she went angling over to a line that would carry her past. But the great disk enlarged and grew greater and they saw seas upon it and clouds and vast areas of green vegetation. When the ship shot past the twilight zone the surface was within mere thousands of miles.

Rod said, "I wish we had a telescope on board. I'm not sure, but I saw some splotches that could be cities."

"Do you think—?"

"I'm not guessing," he told her. "I'm taking a chance. If they beam us it's the pyramid people. If they don't, it isn't. But there must be plenty of civilization in our galaxy. The fact that they had a trick all worked out to get warning when we made space-ships rather hints at that.

"If there are two civilizations there are probably hundreds of thousands. There must be too many for the pyramid people to wipe out, so they only set traps for them and knock them off when they reach a space-ship culture."

Kit said uneasily, "That — ship certainly turned something on us, without trying to signal us first, and we were plainly running away and not trying to fight them."

"Not surprising," said Rod briefly. "I saw the bas-reliefs

they made of humans." The memory of them was clear.

He had. On the pyramid on Calypso there had been modeled human figures. They should have been irresistible as incitements to curiosity, so that the doors would be opened. But the figured people were not modeled by friendly artists. The figures had been made by craftsman who despised their models.

No artist can keep himself out of his work and the figures had actually made Rod angry at the scorn implicit in their making. They pictured humans with strict accuracy but managed somehow to classify them as beasts and vermin. Men would not have pictured men with such scorn.

Rod had felt instant suspicion and hostility toward the builders of the pyramid and was disinclined to do anything they planned for him to do. That was why he'd cut into the pyramid instead of hopefully opening its doors — and that was why there was as yet no warning that humans had achieved space-travel.

Kit said presently, "You're planning to land, Rod. Can we test the air?"

"The sun's the same color as ours at home," Rod told her. "It must have nearly the same spectrum. And the vegetation's green. The chemistry must be the same. If plants use chlorophyl here to utilize sunlight like ours, the air must be oxygen and nitrogen and CO_2. Other gases wouldn't work, we can't even guess at the proportions."

"And the — gravity?" she said uneasily.

"We've nothing to measure it with," he said with a shrug. "But we do know that we didn't have to push unbearably to get over to one side and run past. We practically tested the gravity with our feet — high up as we are." Then he looked at her sharply. "I had some sleep, Kit. I doubt that you did. Better go get some."

She hesitated, and looked at him wistfully. He said heavily, "I'm not very romantic, am I? But I've got plenty on my mind. The people in that space-ship tried to kill us out of hand. They must have killed off the Martians.

"They'll kill not only us but everybody back on Earth if they catch us and find out our physical structure and check it with the records they'll undoubtedly have made when they modeled those figures on the Calypso pyramid. So we've got not only our own lives to think of but literally everybody else's.

"I've got to try to figure out a way to finish this ship, and arm it somehow — but I've got the beginning of an idea — and I've got to concoct some way to blow it and us literally to atoms if we're caught and killed. And after all that I'm — well — I'm very much in love with you and I've got to figure out something to make you safe."

He stood doggedly by the controls, holding the force-field switches against the springs that would throw the *Stellaris* into other-space if he should be killed where he stood. Kit's eyes softened.

"I — see. We can't think about us. Not yet."

"Not yet," he agreed heavily. "If we're safe here — and I'm beginning to think we are — I'm going to try to get the *Stellaris* down. If those splotches are cities the inhabitants may be anything and they may be friendly or not, civilized or not. But I'm hoping they're not the people who tried to kill us."

He turned back to the vision-ports. They were over the night-side of the planet, and to one side—actually it felt as if the planet were below—there was only the blank black bulk of the unknown world. It was hardly a thousand miles away but the *Stellaris* could not be checked to land on it without killing all on board by multiple-gravity deceleration.

Then the dark globe lay behind and it was time to change back to tractor-beams to pull back toward it and lessen the ship's headlong speed toward infinity. And then, hours later, the again-remote planet ceased to dwindle and grew large once more and he juggled alternate tractor and pressor-beams to bring the *Stellaris* close to its day-side, then to match speed with the planet's surface. At long last he dared let the clumsy hulk which was the Earth-ship down into atmosphere

Bellowing came from below "No-o-o-o radar!" And then a new voice called, "No-o-o-o radio!" Because a civilization which did not have space-ships or even radar could have broadcast-waves in its atmosphere, as Earth had done for nearly a hundred years before space-travel became possible to its people.

The ship went heavily lower and lower. more and more slowly in relation to the jungle underneath. Where the ship approached there was jungle. There were rivers. Far away there were the slopes of a mountain range and, off to one side. the authentic blue of a sea. The ship went soggily down and down, its small and accidental crew gazing at the scene no human eyes had ever before looked at—lower still and individual jungle-growths became visible.

There was a straight streak which looked like a highway of some sort. The *Stellaris* floated onward, rocking a little on the pressor-beams which supported it. Then a city appeared at the horizon. There were towers and pinnacles and a myriad prismatic flashings of reflected sunlight.

But there was no movement, no smoke, no aircraft overhead, no signs of alarm or recognition of the *Stellaris'* existence The ship was only two thousand feet up and there were deep depressions in the vegetation below where its pressor-beams touched ground to uphold it.

The city drew near. And it was dead. There was no life anywhere. But it had not been dead long because the jungle had not yet encroached on it. It was simply dead—undevastated. untouched, unharmed but dead.

Rod brought the ship to a wallowing stop over the very center of the metropolis It reached for miles in every direction

On a basis of human occupancy, it could have housed a population of millions. Yet there was no movement below. Rod began painstakingly to let down for a landing in a central open space.

Kit said in a strained voice; "Rod! Those little things on the highway. Colored things! Brightly-colored!"

"My guess," said Rod briefly, "is that they're the inhabitants. People who could build a city like this would be pretty civilized. No reason why they shouldn't wear brightly-colored clothes."

"But they're not moving!"

"My guess," said Rod again, "is that they're dead."

"A plague?"

"No. Our friends," said Rod grimly. "A civilization that could build this city would be close to space-travel. Maybe they sent a ship to that snow-covered planet and found a pyramid there and opened it up to see who among their ancestors had gone there first—and called in our friends to exterminate them."

She stared at him in horror. His face was very white. He nodded toward the very center of the open space into which the *Stellaris* descended. There was a bright metal pyramid there.

"If, by any chance, there was a space-ship off on a voyage when this world was murdered and it came back after the murderers had left," said Rod harshly, "they'd probably think that some survivors had left word for them in that. And they'd open it."

"At a guess that pyramid on Calypso would have killed me too if I'd opened it in the normal way. Very probably that was it. The ones who summoned the murders wouldn't live to know what they'd done or take back any word of what a pyramid implied."

The ship hovered only a hundred feet above the ground. Slowly, slowly, slowly, Rod eased it downward. He expected an impact but the *Stellaris* touched the strange world's surface with a surprising and quite accidental gentleness.

Without explanation Rod went to the air-lock and closed the inner door. He cracked the outer door and sniffed cautiously. He tried again. He took a deep breath. The air seemed to him to be perfectly adequate.

To make sure, he stepped outside and breathed deeply. He felt a bitter amusement at the difference between this instant of landing on a strange world of another sun, and the way he'd pictured it while the *Stellaris* was building.

He hadn't thought that the landing would be made from an almost unmanageable hulk, unequipped for landing or navigation or even the testing of air, lost utterly in space, with the despairing knowledge that probably the best that could be hoped was that the dozen or so humans on the ship might manage to find a place of perpetual exile with a murderous alien race for enemies.

The air was good but nothing else was promising.

If the ship that had contacted the *Stellaris* had reported its encounter a galaxy-wide search for a race attaining space-travel might be already under way. If they found Earth.

For that matter, Earth's cities might already be filled with crumpled figures. Earth's air might already be empty of fliers. Earth's cities might already be as dead as this one. Rod Cantrell looked at tumbled heaps of garments on the pavements about him and cursed thickly.

CHAPTER FIVE

Marks of Murder

IT was one of the girls in charge of the air-purifying plant who solved the food problem for the time being. Her test for toxic substances was simple but absolutely effective. A tiny morsel of vegetation was strapped against a girl's skin near the wrist. A deadly substance would produce immediate re-action. Irritation or pain or loss of sensation would show toxicity without any risk or danger to the girl.

A group of two painters and an arc-welder marched to the edge of the jungle and gathered what fruits they could find. They came back loaded down, reporting apparent cultivation of the ground, only partly overwhelmed with wild growths. Carefully labeled samples decorated the arms of each of the five girls on the ship for the next two hours. Of all the speci-mens, only one produced a slight rash.

Then it was a question of finding out which of the remaining fruits were most palatable. Tiny samples, chewed and swal-lowed, answered that. One produced cramps. The rest seemed good. The problem of food, then, became to some extent merely a matter of gathering a sufficient quantity.

While this went on Rod Cantrell and Kit and one of the ship's electricians went exploring among the city's buildings for equally important materials. They wanted metals, tools, weapons. They hadn't much hope of the last in a civilized city.

They found plenty of metal. They found few tools. What they did find in horrible profusion, though, was the pitiful popu-lation of the city. Garments lay everywhere, each with a heap of dust within it. What unthinkable weapon had killed them could only be guessed at—though Rod thought he had an idea—but surely it had come upon them without warning.

There were huddled heaps of garments in places that were plainly shops, though the show-cases hung from the ceilings. There were innumerable heaps of clothing on the public ways, and in the queer vehicles the oddly human-like dead race had used.

Many of the vehicles were wrecked, as if their drivers had died at the controls and the untended machines had driven on senselessly until they crashed.

There were many quaintly human-like items in the dead civilization. The explorers found one little shop with identifiable cages in it, as if for small captive creatures, and collars of metal apparently intended for pets.

They found where groups of the vanished race had died as if in the midst of friendly conversation and—as their observation grew more acute—they saw that some of the heaps of garments were smaller than others, and that usually such small garments were beside larger ones, as if the murdered children had been with their parents.

Kit grew very pale. Rod glowered as they went on. The electrician with them scowled more and more deeply.

"Who killed all these folks?" he demanded pugnaciously. "It happened all at once an' it couldn't ha' been more'n a couple of years ago."

"I think," said Rod tonelessly, "it was the gang we ran away from. The gang that made a metal pyramid on Calypso. The same gang that built a metal pyramid not far from where I landed the ship— which we're going to make use of if we have luck."

The electrician spat. "An' you think they killed these people?"

"Because," Rod told him, "they made a space-ship. The pyramid on Calypso was supposed to tip them off when we did. The pyramid in the square back by the ship is bait. If there was a space-ship away from home when this world was killed and if it came back, the people in it would think some survivors of the catastrophe had left a record for them."

"They'd go inside to see. And they'd be killed. *And* the murderers would be notified to come and mop up just to make sure. See?"

The electrician spat again. "We'd better figure out something to slap them guys down," he said coldly. "They need it."

The three went on. And everywhere they moved through the city they saw new evidences of the high degree of civilization the dead race had achieved, more and more of the pathetic heaps of garments which had been members of that race. Kit, perhaps, saw those most clearly. The electrician saw also the enormous wealth left ownerless by the annihilation of its creators.

Not only was there a metropolis left, which humans could take over and use with little modification, but there were goods and even jewels—strangely-cut and very beautiful—and all the other portable possessions of a civilized world. He made no move to burden himself though. There was too much of riches in sight to make mere looting a temptation. But it was plain enough that he saw.

Rod saw the technical side of the murdered culture. He noted the lavish use of non-corrodible alloys. He saw plastics used where human-made plastics would not have been satisfactory. He took a small sliver of colorless transparent stuff and held a flame to it. It did not discolor or char.

"Looks like fluocarbon," he said absorbedly. "These people had gone places!"

Then they entered a great building which was plainly a power-station and a communication-center at once. Here Rod was in his element and the electrician was not far behind him. The central hall was huge and bright with sunlight and there were many machines upon the floor.

"Generator yonder," said Rod, nodding. "Looks like an electron-emitting isotope trick like ours. See the power-leads from it?"

The electrician observed, "Silver bus-bars. Looks like nylon insulation everywhere."

"Or fluocarbon plastic. Hm." Rod stared at a huge block of solid transparent stuff with metal sheets and rods deeply imbedded in it. Power-leads ran to it but the metal sheets did not connect within the transparency. He stared while the others wandered about. Then Kit, a little distance away, uttered a cry.

"Rod! Come here! Oh—it's terrible!"

Rod went quickly. And Kit was standing with clenched hands before a double row of instruments. Between them the floor was quite covered with the bright garments of the dead race, showing that all the occupants of the building had been crowded here when death fell upon their city. And the rows of instruments showed why.

They were, in effect, television instruments. But it took time to realize it, because on each screen a distinct and motionless image remained. Each instrument still showed the picture that had been upon it at the instant the city died.

Some of the pictures were of individual members of the race in the act of speaking. Others—many others—were of scenes upon the ways, either of this city or another, showing the dead race as it had been. On two screens there was no hint of danger or of the coming of death.

But no less than six showed the death-agonies of those who were still not dead. The screens were horrible to look at. Three —and this was where the heaps of garments were thickest— showed the sky. Each showed a strange object against a background of clouds or stars. And the three were identical. Each was a monstrous metal pryamid.

Rod stared woodenly at the images. Then he examined the instruments which held them.

"Vision-screens," he announced unnecessarily. Then he added, "A good trick. They didn't project their television. They modified a plate of some sort that can change like—well—like the skin of a chameleon. Didn't have to worry about brightness. Like a photograph, only it must have moved. When the machine went off the last picture stayed until it went back on again."

He fumbled and peeled off a strip of flexible material which formed the screen. The image remained on it. It was, in effect, a photograph of the last object the dying eyes of these people

had looked at. He hunted and found a stock of similar sheets
—but blank—to be used as replacements.

"Television," he said, "only you could keep any scene you
wanted to as a photograph. I think I've got a good hunch on
what killed these people. The trouble is to prove it."

Kit caught her breath. She was grief-stricken at the pictures.

"Rod! They were so much like us! So *much* like us!"

"That flying pryamid was the destroyer," Rod pointed out.
"A pyramid's a good structural form—the most rigid you can
make with straight girders. And there's no sense in stream-
lining a space-ship because there's no air-resistance in space.
Besides, polished metal at such angles would reflect away radar-
beams—solar heat too if they wanted to go close to a sun.

"My guess is that was a fighting-ship. It appeared in the
sky overhead and these people's telescopes picked it up and
they were watching it when they died."

The electrician said suddenly, "*Hey!* These sets must've
blown out—"

"Whatever killed the people stopped the sets," agreed Rod
coldly. "They wouldn't have switched them off just because
they were dying. Whatever killed the people did something to
the sets! If we open one up we may check on an idea I've got."

He saw the electrician reach in his overall pocket for tools.
He went to the big block of plastic with the imbedded and covered metal plates. The thing bothered him. The plastic was
plainly an insulator and as plainly the whole thing was designed
to perform some electrostatic or electronic function. He felt
that he ought to understand.

One of the plates wasn't solid metal but pierced with innumerable holes like a sieve. Rod frowned, a hunch telling him
that this was important. He tried to figure it out as an electrostatic device, guessing at capacity-effects between the enclosed
plates. But this part would neutralize the capacity-effect between that and that and—

His mouth dropped open. It was a vacuum tube! Save that the parts were imbedded in plastic instead of held in emptiness, it was plainly a vacuum tube! The plastic must have acted electronically like a vacuum, allowing electron-flow. And they must have had the trick of cold emission of electrons from a metal surface! If that were so this device would handle incredible amounts of power!

As Rod's eyes began to glow, the electrician came to him. "*Hey!* We can fix these sets! I opened one up and a pair of porcelain insulators is crumpled all up. They were the mounting insulators and they went to powder and the works settled and shorted and quit workin'!"

Rod wanted to babble of his own discovery but instead he followed back to the vision-sets. It was as the electrician had said. Supports for the apparatus within the cases had shivered to powder.

Kit had a strange expression on her face.

"Rod! I've got an idea. I don't know anything about science but in school once our instructor showed us how supersonic waves could break glass to powder if they were strong enough and of sufficient high-frequency. He said they were used to sterilize things. Could the way these people were killed be something like that?"

"It could," said Rod grimly. "We had a dose of something like it from that other space-ship—remember? But air won't carry supersonics. It's elastic and they go down in pitch. And there wasn't any air where that other space-ship caught up with us. I think you're close. Very close."

The electrician showed Kit the powder remaining from the shattered insulators. It was very fine. The rest of the insulation was plastic. Then he bent down and tore at silken garments on the floor. Not even Kit protested. The dead race had no such bony skeletons as humanity possesses. There was only fine dust within the garments. The electrician folded torn cloth to a pad.

"This's dry," he observed. "It'd ought to do for a insulator for a try, anyhow."

He reached into the case, then drew back and put on rubber gloves for safety's sake. As he lifted the settled mass of coils and wires there was a tiny snapping sound. A spark jumped brittlely and ceased. The electrician put the pad in place. He prepared another and adjusted that.

Kit said tensely, "It's working!"

They looked. The sheet on which a colored photograph had appeared permanently fixed now changed beneath their eyes. It was extraordinary to see the picture, by the light from overhead, change itself by an apparent flow of pigment from one spot to another to form a new arrangement of shapes and colors.

Where the scene on this instrument's screen had been that of the last instant in the life of the people of this planet, now it was the scene currently in being. The street was empty of moving forms but there were those empty heaps of garments on the ground where the people of the planet had been. It was plainly a current view of the place where the connected sending instrument stood.

· And then, preposterously, as they watched there came a movement in the distance. Kit caught her breath. Then the electrician swore luridly. And then Rod clenched his hands until the blood flowed in his palms.

CHAPTER SIX

Pyramids Coming!

THERE were living creatures moving toward the sending-instrument. Not many—the three human watchers could see clearly and there were but four individuals in sight. Those four individuals rode in one of the odd vehicles native to the planet. Rod and the others watched intently.

They had bulbous heads and attenuated arms and legs, and one of them guided the vehicle to a spot no more than fifty or sixty yards from the vision-sender. There the vehicle stopped. The four got out and stared at a building.

One lifted something from a belt about his middle. Flame darted from it in a thin straight line. He swept it up, and side-wise, and down, and across again. A section of plastic-sealed wall fell slowly outward.

From somewhere within the vision-instrument, they heard the crash of its fall. The four marched unconcernedly across the wreckage, trampling underfoot the gay garments of the murdered native race.

Rod said in a whisper, "This may be a sender too. No noise!"

The three humans stood motionless. In minutes the four stick-like figures came out, burdened with loads of shimmering stuff the watchers could not identify. They piled it in the vehicle. They went back as if for more.

Rod thrust the others from before the vision-machine so that, if this were a two-way instrument, their images would not remain on the screen at the other end. Crisply he ripped out the pads of temporary insulation. There was a tiny spark and the picture ceased to move.

"They're looters," said Rod grimly. "They're not the native race certainly. Presumably they're the crowd that travels in those flying pyramids. They're the murderers. And now it be-comes clear why they wait for another race to reach the space-ship stage of civilization before they murder them.

"A civilized race leaves a civilization behind when it dies. It leaves cities to be looted. It turns murder from a precaution into a business!" His nostrils were widened. He breathed heavily, went white with a deep, corrosive anger.

"We go back to the ship," he said flatly. "You see the pattern! They murdered the natives of this planet without warning and set up at least one pyramid to tell them if any survivors turned up later.

"When they were sure it was quite safe they came back and now they've begun the leisurely looting of the cities whose inhabitants they killed. Quite safe and very logical."

His tone, at the end, changed to raging fury. But he led the way back toward the ship without a word of explanation. He was torn between quite irrational rage and a desperate desire to get Kit away from here and out of danger. Yet he knew that even back on Earth, unless something quite impossible happened, Kit would be equally doomed. Whether in flight through space or hidden in the dark universe she was in no better case.

Through the air-lock and into the ship. The party gone to gather fruit was back with a large supply. Rod called a meeting of the curiously-assorted ship's company. He curtly summed up the situation.

"There are three things we can do," he said shortly at the end. "We can leave this planet, which is being looted by the creatures who killed its inhabitants. That means taking a chance we can't even estimate of finding another planet where we can try to provision ourselves — and possibly arm ourselves for defense.

"We can go into the dark universe and open the air-lock and die quickly. Or —" he paused — "we can stay here, fight or dodge the looters and try to find an observatory and star-maps and possibly the way back home."

There could be no dissension. But a painter pointed out that since he hadn't agreed to this voyage he considered that he was on overtime — rather, double-time pay for all work done outside of his regular job of painting. His union, in fact, might insist on a still higher rate of pay. And he would work only if assured that a mediation-based award of pay would be accepted.

Rod agreed impatiently.

"But the first thing," he said urgently, "is to hide the ship. The only safe hiding-place is the dark universe. You know how the field-generators were tested. We anchored the ship in place with focused tractor-beams and then turned on the fields. She went into the dark universe, but stayed in the part of it parallel to her slip. When the fields were turned off she came back to where she'd been. That's what we'll have to do now."

One of the girl biologists said dismally, "No weight?"

"No weight," agreed Rod. "Except for those of us out on the planet, working a little trick I think we can handle. Who volunteers for that?"

He had his pick of the ship's company. He chose an electrician and a painter and almost angrily refused Kit's insistence that she be of the party.

"I'm not going to take any chances," he told her, "but I don't want to be worried about you. And you're more able than anybody else to attend to what has to be done — on the ship, that is."

He shifted the *Stellaris* on her pressor-beams to a position close by the walls of a massive building. He anchored her there by focused beams and flicked on the force-fields for the infinitesimal part of a second. Back in normal space the ship had not moved. He tried it again for longer periods.

The anchoring tractors worked exactly as he wished. Focused, they worked even from the other-space, though when unfocused they could not be used either into or out of it. He wrote, at some length. Then he took a half-dozen small objects and focused material-handler tractor beams on them — small beams. He turned the tractor-power away down and then took them out of the ship despite the reduced-power tractor's pull.

He wedged them in place so they could not fly back to the ship until released but so that they would fly back to the ship, even into the dark universe, when set free. Then he was ready. He and his two followers went outside. Rod looked up to the port through which Kit regarded him anxiously. He waved his hand.

There was a puff of air. The *Stellaris* — was not. There was only emptiness where she had been. She was in another cosmos, in another set of dimensions, as far removed from this planet's surface as the farthest island universe.

Yet if any of the small objects arranged for the purpose were released it would be drawn to the ship and through the forcefield and into the open air-lock in the fraction of a second, implying a removal of no more than yards.

Rod started off for the big building in which he'd found the television sets and the isotopic generator and the huge mass of plastic which was a vacuum tube in its functioning. On the way he spoke crisply.

"We had a space-ship turn something on us that was pretty bad. It lasted only the fraction of a second, so it didn't kill us. Here something deadly hit. It didn't break plastic or metal or stone but it crumbled ceramic insulators to powder. Got any idea what it could be?"

The painter, knitting his brows, said, "You can break china when plastic only bounces. What they got? Something that smacks hard?"

"They didn't push down the buildings," Rod pointed out. "A bunch of little blows, like a compressed-air drill, will cut through stone that a straight push or a rotary drill won't handle. My guess is they had a sort of pressor-beam, only instead of pushing steadily it hit hard and fast — and often. Vibration."

The electrician said, demurring, "Y'd get an awful kick-back from a pressor-beam that went off an' on like that!"

"Suppose," said Rod, "in between it was a tractor? Suppose they had a beam that changed from a pressor to a tractor a hundred times a second — two hundred thousand? What then?"

The three men took half a dozen steps toward the hall of the machines and television sets. Then the electrician grunted.

"Mmmh! You could fix the tensor-plate to be a chopper! Migawd, yeah! *Say!* I could fix one o' them!"

"We're going to," said Rod curtly. "We're going to use something the people that built this city made. My guess is that it'll handle a few hundred million kilowatts. And I know a power-unit that'll give it that much power—for awhile. We're going to work like hades!"

In his mind there was a feeling of terrible urgency. There were looters in some other city of this same planet. That meant there was a pyramid-ship here too. It might be the plan of the space-murderers to loot one city of this planet at a time. It was much more likely that there would be cargoships coming to load up with the booty of their crime at as many cities as possible.

They'd have waited until they felt it safe to loot — but once they began they would not want the looting to spread over a term of years. After all, the jungle would begin to creep into the dead cities. Since there were already looters in one city there should be others on the way.

The electrician set about gathering the material for his coils and plates, cutting away freely at bus-bars and cables of solid silver to supply his needs. With power such as Rod had spoken of no mere wire would serve as conductors. He cut and tugged and tugged and cut.

Rod and the painter went out to hunt for a vehicle that could be made to run. When they found one not outwardly wrecked Rod had to sweat over it to discover how it ran. It stirred feebly — and that was all. They tried a second and its power was dead.

It was not until they came upon one which had apparently waited for its owners or passengers beneath an overhanging arch — so that it was protected from rain — that the queer vehicle moved briskly. Then they had to learn to guide it.

But they were back and trundling into the great hall before the electrician had begun to shape those illogical and super-ficially insane twistings of metal which ordinarily are hidden by weather-proof housings and careful range-limiters, in the tractor and pressor-beams of commerce.

He stopped to help Rod make sure of the cutting-off of the isotopic generator and then the two of them hacked at heavy leads and struggled with the massive bus-bars they would require. The painter judgmatically contrived a way to load the big block of plastic — which was a vacuum tube — on the vehicle. Then Rod and the electrician mounted their coils about the "tube" in its exotic placing.

"I've got a hunch," said Rod suddenly. "This is our mount! We'll run it up to the pyramid, cut in and connect the leads with the power-unit there. And then —"

The electrician swung around suddenly. "Yeah!" he said, blankly. "*Then! Lookaheah!* This thing ain't got any guides! I got her hooked to squeal up to the bloopin' point, an' with enough power in her there ain't goin' to be anything in who knows how far ain't goin' to hot up! Where're we goin' to be when you turn her on?"

"On the ship," said Rod, "and in the dark universe. We'll be safe there. I've got an idea how bad this is going to be!"

He worked on, grimly. Hours passed. Sweat covered him. The electrician mopped his forehead from time to time. The painter helped awkwardly, obeying orders. The feeling of tenseness grew greater and greater in Rod's mind. It was un-reasonable but it was overpowering. It was a hunch so strong that at last he dared not wait longer.

"We get going," he said brittlely. "I'd like to file it down a little more but we can't risk it. Come along!"

He started the little vehicle. He ran it slowly out of the building, then faster and ever faster to the square where the

Stellaris had landed. He backed it to the base of the pyramid
— which was so much like that one on Calypso — save that
the bas-reliefs pictured another race than the human — and
stopped the vehicle.

He ran across the square to where he had wedged certain
small objects in place. He scribbled a note to Kit on a scrap
of paper as he ran. The paper was the order removing him
from authority over the *Stellaris*. With an almost hysterical
sensation of urgency he jammed the note into the little object,
which pulled and tugged to escape from his hand.

He released it.

It flashed through the air — and vanished. It had been
drawn through the force-field which cut off all the rest of the
universe of stars from the *Stellaris*. It had, unquestionably,
gone into other-space and clanked loudly in the open air-lock
door of the space-ship.

And Rod stood wrestling with his illogical impatience while
seconds ticked away, more seconds and more — but he had
given strict orders that when a noise of an arriving object
sounded in the air-lock, the outer door was to be closed and
the object examined for a note before any action was taken.

Then — there was the *Stellaris* before him, come out of another set of dimensions and another universe to obey his orders.

He rushed into the air-lock, shaking with the feeling of im-
minent need. "A torch!" he commanded feverishly. "A cutting-
torch! Make it quick! Speed! For the love of —"

He took the tiny, deadly instrument and raced back with it.
He began fiercely to cut through the plating of the pyramid
which was intended to kill any who opened it in the obvious
way and signal the tampering to a race of killers. The metal
smoked and a thin line of parting showed. He cut through
swiftly, counting somehow upon the inner identity of this
pyramid to the other he had opened.

It was identical. He crawled inside, dragging the torch,

scorching his clothing and legs on the hot edges he had cut. Again he cut at metal ruthlessly. He snapped commands and the electrician fed in one long section of bus-bar. He welded it to a connection. He welded a second semi-flexible bar.

He backed out and barked to the painter to get a string, a plumb-line, anything that was cord. And not to let anybody come out of the ship! Even as he commanded he was feverishly using the torch to connect the snaky bus-bars from the pyramid's interior to the preposterous-seeming device mounted on the odd small vehicle.

He finished and cast aside the torch to attach the string with unreasonably shaking fingers to the switch which was so ingenious and so easy to throw and would handle so monstrous a current.

"Okay," he barked. "Get back and in the ship! *Run!*"

He backed toward the *Stellaris* himself, paying out the string.

Then he heard Kit crying out. *"Rod—Pyramids!"*

Out of the corner of his eye he saw a mote in the sky at the edge of the horizon. But he dared not hasten. He paid out the string and paid it out. He stripped off his coat and knotted the end of the string to it. Then he ran.

Ther were voices babbling about him as he focused a tractor-beam on his coat, a hundred feet away. With the least possible trace of power he saw the cloth stir.

"Go ahead!" he roared.

He stared out the vision-port. There was not one pyramid in sight but three. They came drifting onward and downward, lower, toward the city. The *Stellaris* must be visible. They would turn their beams on it as a mere routine precaution.

All visible things turned red, flashed through all the colors of the spectrum to violet and dead-black. The *Stellaris* was in other-space, the dark universe.

Then Rod raised the power on the tractor-beam, drawing

his coat toward him in another set of dimensions. He heard a faint tinking sound — the coat's metal buttons were smacking forcibly against the ship's hull.

Then Rod wanted to be sick — from relief.

CHAPTER SEVEN

Ambush

TIME passed slowly indeed in the other-space. Rod found himself doubting the time-rate of his watch. But a watch did keep the same time in the dark universe as in normal space. He knew it. It had been verified on his three interplanetary trips and in the original testings of the *Stellaris* when her force-field coils were first tried out. But the watch hands moved slowly, very slowly.

Kit looked at him with anxious eyes. There were lights in the ship now but the feeling of weightlessness kept a certain nagging impulse of panic always very close. Still, Kit had been so much more fearful for Rod that the eerie sensation of floating in emptiness could almost be ignored, now that he was safe on board.

"What'd you do, Rod?" she asked.

"I think," said Rod, "that I knocked off the looters and the creatures in the three flying pyramids we saw. I hope so! I even think I did it with one of their own weapons. I hope very much that they haven't any defense against it. I can't imagine one."

"*Their weapons?*" Kit said, startled. "You mean you think you made the same thing they used to kill all the people on this planet?"

"And the Martians," said Rod grimly, "and probably plenty of other races that got civilized enough to be either dangerous or worth looting. Remember, you suggested that the weapon a space-ship turned on us might be supersonic-sound waves?"

"Y-yes," said Kit uneasily.

"It couldn't have been exactly sound-waves. Not in space. There was no air — or any solid to carry them. But we use tractor beams as if they were cables to pull things and pressors as if they were beams to push things with. I figured that they might have made a gadget that alternated between sending tractor and pressor beams.

"It would send a thin slice of tractor, then a thin slice of pressor and so on. That would go through space. And when it hit something solid it would generate sound waves in it. If the slices were thin enough and alternated fast enough they'd make supersonic waves — such as you suggested — in anything they touched.

"Air would vibrate in the supersonic range. So would water. So would the bodies of any living creatures such a beam struck. It would break up ceramic ware and not break plastic or metal. Sent from one space-ship to another, it would kill all the crew of the ship on the receiving end. Sent from a ship down on a city —"

Kit turned pale.

"They could — stay out in space and send beams down at a city and everybody'd die! Oh, Rod!"

"Apparently they did just that," said Rod. "Anyhow, that's the sort of gadget I made. There were bus-bars and a monstrous thing that works like a vacuum-tube in the building where we saw the televisors.

"Joe and I — Joe's the electrician who was with us — fixed up a pressor-beam generator and put in a feed-back to the tensor-plate. It starts to make pressors, the feed-back makes it shift to tractors, then the feed-back makes it shift back to pressors and so on. It'll generate supersonic frequencies all right! Simple enough too," he added grimly.

"But —"

"Power for it? There was an isotopic generator in the building with the televisors, too. Probably better than the one we have on the ship here. But I did better than that. I knew there ought to be a power-storage unit in the booby-trap pyramid we so carefully haven't touched.

"I cut into that pyramid, hooked up that power to the gadget Joe and I had put together and tied a string to the switch. I focused a tractor to pull the string after we'd come into this space. The stuff it generated couldn't hurt us here. Tractor and pressor stuff would have to be focused to come into this universe from ours."

He made an unconscious movement and rather absurdly floated away from his former position. There was no gravity here. There was always the sensation of interminable fall. While constantly aware of the fact that it was weightlessness, not dropping, it was endurable enough. But nobody would ever be able to sleep where gravity was not.

"To finish the picture," said Rod after a moment, "the power-storage unit has probably some hundreds of millions of kilowatts of power stored in it. I don't know just how fast it'll discharge through our gadget but there's a choke-effect there to slow it up.

"My guess and my hope is that my gadget generated the pyramid-folks pet murder-frequency stuff for several successive minutes and that those who happened to be around have lost all interest in looting — and in us."

"If it hit them," said Kit.

"It did," he assured her. "We set it to radiate in all directions. The faster the juice ran out, the more deadly that beam was. I can't guess its maximum range but it should be strong enough anywhere on this planet!"

In that estimate he was too conservative. Actually the lethal effect of his device had extended rather more than a planetary diameter beyond the surface on the far side of the world. It had lasted for six or seven minutes and it had wiped out all pyramid-creatures within that limit.

Rod, however, was uneasy. His experience of the alien race was not enough to let him know their resources, and he could not calibrate or measure anything he used.

At the moment he worried mainly over the possibility that the aliens might have some defense against the weapon he thought they used for massacres. But he knew, too, that the danger could be greater than that and of a quite different sort.

As a matter of safety he kept the *Stellaris* in other-space for twelve hours. If the aliens had a defense against his weapon they'd expect the *Stellaris* to reappear immediately the weapon was used. But if twelve full hours elapsed they would think the human ship had fled. So he waited.

But time passed very slowly until what might be termed social life within the ship began. The four girls who'd tended the air-purifier system had been classed officially as assistants in biology, and were more or less inclined to feel superior to mere painters and arc-welders and electricians. Some of the men, too, were middle-aged and obviously family men.

But one of the arc-welders was good looking and one of the painters displayed virtuosity on the mouth-organ. Also there was some food aboard ship and there was at least a precedent for expecting to set foot again on a planet with breathable air.

Also there were the lurid tales of riches and jewels and incredible luxury in the empty cities of the planet to which they were still anchored. So, during the tedious wait, barriers broke. Music began somewhere off in the ship. There were voices. There was even laughter.

Kit went to see while Rod sweatingly tried to make calculations and draw diagrams on a memo-pad which had no weight — and while he himself floated head-down in relation to a normal position in the control-room. Kit drew herself lightly along the hand-rails which ran on floors and ceilings and side-walls alike. She came back smiling, floating with extraordinary grace in mid-air.

"Rod! You ought to see!" she told him. "One of the painters has tied himself in place with string. He's playing the mouth-organ and they're having a dance! It's like a Virginia reel in three dimensions! Everybody's got pieces of cardboard and they're using them like wings to fan themselves around with in the craziest set-to you ever saw!"

Uproarious laughter sounded in the ship, which floated in an illimitable emptiness of darkness — in a universe in which no living thing could dwell — alone as surely no human ship was ever alone before — in a cosmos without a single star.

Rod said restlessly, "That's good, Kit. Go and watch if you like. I'd better not. Anyhow, I'm going to try something."

There was reason for his reserve. He was, perforce, the captain of the *Stellaris*. As such he could join in difficult labor and should share in any danger. But he must remain remote if all his decisions were to go unquestioned. And it was necessary for him to make the decisions. If he relaxed to mere sociable behavior his leadership would no longer be based upon the mystery of commissioned authority. He would have become merely another man.

He pulled himself to the engine-room. Restlessly he set the tractor-beams — those not in use for anchorage — to fan out in all directions through this other-space. Practically nothing was known as yet about the dark universe. Light traveled faster there and inertia was less. Incredible speeds were possible.

So much was known, and nothing else. The other-space could be a mere incalculable emptiness, without the most minute particle of substance anywhere in it. Yet in theory a cosmos without mass could not exist. A closed universe could not be closed without substance to make the gravitational warp that would close it. So there must be matter of some sort.

But Rod turned on the tractor-beams and fanned them out, merely to be doing something. The odds against any solid object within the distance the tractor-beams would cross within a few hours — even at the tremendous speed of radiation here were enormous.

He went back to the control-room, looking at his watch. Kit rested lightly in a screwed-down chair, staring at nothing. Her face was utterly dismal.

"I — er — I put on the tractor-beams to see if there could be anything solid around," he told her, pretending not to see her expression.

She did not answer.

"I'm hoping," he said awkwardly after a moment, "that we've wiped out those pyramid-makers and that we'll be able to go through one of their ships and pick up some of their stuff. In this space those projectors of theirs that shoot beams of light should be handy. I'd like to know what kind of drive they have — and they've got a sort of flame-pistol that could be useful."

Kit's lips trembled. A tear appeared at the corner of her eye and did not run down her cheek because there was no gravity to draw it. It blurred all her vision and she shook her head to clear it. The tear-drop flew off into the air as a tiny round globule. She gulped.

Rod said helplessly, "I feel like a scoundrel, Kit. I act as if I didn't think about you at all."

"You don't think of me," said Kit. "And — and we're likely to be killed any time and —"

"If you looked happy," said Rod doggedly, "as if we were being romantic, the four other girls would envy you. And if romance breaks out in this ship it will be bad! There are ten men and only five girls. Right now it doesn't look as if we've much chance of getting back and if ten men get romantic over five girls —"

"S-some of the men are m-married," said Kit.

"It'll be hard for them to bear that in mind after they give up hope of getting back home and know they're some thousands of light-years away."

Then Rod said grimly, "I look at it this way — we're in the position of people who were shipwrecked in the olden days. But we've no hope of being rescued. No friendly space-ship will ever run across us! So we've got to load up with food. We've got to get weapons. We've got to get tools.

"And if we can't find our way back to Earth — the chance is slim — we've got to find a planet these space-murderers aren't interested in, one that we can settle on. We may have to turn ourselves into a colony and spend all our lives somewhere we can't even guess at yet. Right now we've got to keep from doing anything that will start dissension on board."

"You could say something nice once in a while," said Kit miserably.

"If I did," said Rod, "I wouldn't want to stop at that."

The ship stirred — slightly but definitely.

Rod dived for the corridor to the engine-room. The movement of the ship could mean but one thing. The tractor-beam had touched something solid. Even hurtling through the air he glanced at his watch. The beam had been on for fourteen minutes. That would mean a hundred and sixty million miles in normal space. It might mean ten or twenty or a hundred times that, here. It might mean anything or nothing whatever.

He reached the beam-projectors. Again carefully leaving the anchor-tractors untouched, Rod cut down the power of one after another of the rest. Another stirring. The beam which had struck something was identified. He put pressors in parallel and sent them out to cover the direction.

It was again fourteen minutes before a pressor hit the unseen object the tractor tugged at. Rod took a deep breath. It wasn't coming this way, then. Not fast at any rate.

He settled down to finicky, delicate manipulation. It was, in a way, ridiculous for him to try to locate and focus a beam on something of unknown size — an unguessable but enormous distance away — when it was somewhere in a fifteen-degree-square arc of space.

It took fourteen minutes to discover whether an individual beam was even pointed in the right direction. But he had a dozen beams he could use, adjusting them in sequence, and he could shift the unfocused beams to find when they slid off the object.

The three-dimensional dance ended when the painter ran out of breath with which to blow the harmonica. An impromptu theatrical performance began. There was a painter who fancied himself as a tap-dancer. He essayed to demonstrate. With no weight to hold him anywhere his antics were unpredictable even to himself.

The spectators held fast to handrails on walls and floor and ceiling. The girls shrieked with laughter. The men howled. Somebody essayed to juggle. It was impossible. Nothing came back to his hands. The laughter tended to grow hysterical.

It was a wholesome enterprise and it was all very well as long as they could remember that they were not falling into endless nothingness. These antics helped them to remember. But the instant that thought ceased to hold the center of one's mind, muscles tensed in panic, eyes widened and breathing became difficult because one was falling, falling, falling. . . .

It was long hours before Rod heard the curious crisp noise within a pressor-coil which told that it was locked. It was focused upon something invisible and unspeakably remote in the absolute black of other-space. Rod looked at the beam-mounting. He made a tiny mark. After half an hour, there was no change in the long-range adjustment. Whatever the object was, it had no great velocity either toward or away from the *Stellaris*.

If it was a — well — a heavenly body, a burned-out sun in a universe run down, it might be useful. So Rod left a beam on it, drawing the minimum of power. He went floating along the corridor to the control-room and there Kit looked at him steadily, a sheet of paper in her hand. She no longer looked unhappy.

"Rod," she said, "do you remember writing this?"

Rod flushed. He'd written her a note before going out to make the death-beam generator. The *Stellaris* was to vanish from the planet's surface while he worked — it was to hide in other-space because there were alien looters on the unnamed world.

Pyramid-ships might come to this city. They might beam any area they intended to land on, as a matter of routine precaution. If they did he and the other two men on the planet's surface would die. So he'd written a note for Kit to find in case he didn't come back. And she'd found it.

"I didn't think to tear that up when I came back," he said uncomfortably. "Just — well — forget it, won't you?"

"Hardly!" said Kit. She smiled tremulously. "If you really feel this way about me, I want to remember it. I won't doubt any more!"

She smiled at him. The temptation was irresistible. But the electrician named Joe came floating into the control-room, flapping two large sheets of cardboard for wings. He braked expertly with them and grinned.

"If I only had a harp," he said, beaming, "I'd feel like an angel for sure!"

"I'm getting set to go back and see what our trick did to those looters and the pyramid-ships," Rod told him, momentarily confused.

Joe raised his eyebrows and made no comment. He fanned himself to a wall and caught hold of a hand-rail.

"I'd like to spring an idea," he said.

"Go ahead!"

"Suppose we fix up a couple gizmos like the one we made back yonder on the planet," said Joe. "Then we could put up a scrap if one of them pyramids came after us."

"Providing we shot first," said Rod.

"That's right," agreed Joe. "But suppose we tricked the circuit so the tensor-plate was choked? So when we turned on the juice nothin' happened?"

Rod waited, frowning.

"Then," said Joe, grinning, "if they turned a beam on us, our feed-backs 'ud pick it up an' uncork our beam on them! They start shootin', an' automatic we shoot back."

"Good enough," admitted Rod. "Only we'd still die. That wouldn't kill their beams. It would just kill them."

"Then tie in our force-field switch," said Joe amiably. "They slap a beam on us, we shoot back an' go whammo into other-space. All automatic! A bear-trap. I don't like those guys!"

"I don't either," said Rod. He reflected. "Mmmmmm. You've got something there. I begin to like it. I wonder if they have it."

"It's not likely, Rod," Kit interposed. "They'll kill off other civilizations as soon as they have space-travel. You didn't arm your first ship and there was no plan to arm the *Stellaris*. Nobody'd be set to fight in their first space-ships.

"The pyramid-people have probably never had a real fight in their lives. They won't be looking for anybody to fight back, any more than a hunter expects a rabbit to let go at him with a blaster."

"Something there too," admitted Rod. "But they're probably scary at that. Most likely they started this murder business because they were frightened the first time their ships came upon another race. They wiped that race out because it scared them. Then they looted its cities and found it paid off. Still, if they think that way . . ."

A chilly thought came to him. He felt small cold prickles running up and down his spine.

"Right now we've got to take a chance that we hit them hard," he said grimly. "Pass along the word that we're going back to normal space on the planet we found. And Joe —"

"Yeah?"

"Go down in the engine-room. I've got a pressor locked on something in the dark universe. If I throw the force-fields back on, you put power into that pressor. Plenty of it! We'll want to get moving, and fast!"

Joe grinned, let go of the hand-rail and flapped blissfully across the room. He bounced off the doorway and went soaring toward the engines.

Shoutings went through the ship. There was a roll-call, so that the sudden return of gravity would not take anyone by surprise. Then Rod threw off the force-fields.

Weight came back, but no light outside. Rod blinked, then roared, "Lights out! *Quick!*" It was night outside on the planet, and the lighted ports of the *Stellaris* would show for miles.

After long minutes Rod put Kit's hands on the switch that would send the *Stellaris* back to other-space. Quietly — it seemed strange to be able to walk — he went to the air-lock. He cracked it open. There was no sound anywhere. He stepped out into the night. The air was chill and many strange stars shone overhead. It was altogether eerie to stand in such strangeness on the ways of a city that had been murdered, on a planet that had no name, in the weird stillness of its night.

But night had not long fallen. On the horizon there was still a trace of luminosity. A single wisp of cloud, high up, glowed faintly in sunlight from below the horizon. But overhead the sky was deep-blue. Stars twinkled brightly.

And there was silence to crack the eardrums. Perhaps at the edge of the city where the jungle began, boughs and branches whispered in a night-wind. But here all was stillness. Every-

thing was dead. As his eyes adjusted to the starlight the soaring, graceful architecture took form in the dimness.

And then he saw one of the pyramids that had been floating
overhead before the *Stellaris* — its improvisioned weapon radi-
ating death — had fled into the other-space. The pyramid had
come down out of control.

It had crashed into the side of a cliff-like structure and
tumbled out again. It lay askew with one of its corners still
caught in the gap its impact had made. Rod drew a deep
breath of satisfaction. The weapon he'd made had worked.
There was now no living alien of the murderous race upon
this planet. But —

Something made him raise his eyes. Stars moved overhead.
They moved visibly. Tiny specks of yellow incandescence
shifted place among the many-colored distant suns. One winked
out completely. Another suddenly appeared.

For an instant Rod thought of shooting stars — of meteors.
But meteors do not move slowly. These things did. Especially,
meteors do not move in geometric formation, arranged as a
slightly skewed triangle which give the appearance from one
viewpoint of a pyramid.

The specks were pyramid-ships — a space-fleet of the killer-
race! There were literally hundreds of them and they approached the planet on which Rod stood. The flashes of light
were sunlight reflected from their polished sides.

Rod went cold all over. But it was obvious enough, once he
thought about it. The aliens who put up a pyramid on Calypso
had the mentality of people who install elaborate burglar-
alarms. It was part of a pattern of thought.

They did not think of mercy, so they would not think of
watchfulness. Cold-bloodedness manifesting itself in unwarned
race-murders implied a whole psychology. And a suspicion that
had come to Rod no more than half an hour since was verified.

The aliens plainly took no chances. As they did not imagine

friendly commerce — implying loyalty — between different races, they did not imagine loyalty or courage in their own. So a pyramid-ship was not trusted to meet and report upon emergencies.

As a power-storage unit and a transmitter was built into the traps they set for other civilizations, so similar devices were built into their ships. In the unthinkable event that one of their crews was wiped out by a race unknown to them the crew was not depended on to report with their last trace of strength.

When the stick-like creatures in a pyramid-ship died the ship itself sent out a death-cry of radiation which could travel across half a galaxy. Perhaps there were relays to receive and transmit communications faster than the speed of light. When a ship was destroyed, a monstrous, overwhelming fleet could be sent instantly to avenge and destroy.

The winking spects of light moved on. Probably they would englobe the planet on which the looting-party had been destroyed. They might blast the planet itself out of existence. Or perhaps —

Rod ground his teeth. He'd made a mistake. He'd lost precious hours out of exaggerated caution. But he would not make that mistake again.

He went back into the ship to give crisp and savage orders.

CHAPTER EIGHT

The Enemy

THERE was no alarm but the suspense itself was hair-raising. Joe the electrician and an arc-welder with a torch cut loose the generator of the deadly tractor-pressor radiation. Already there was a tendency to call it "the push-pull beam" instead of tractor-pressor or supersonic radiation.

While they did so Rod and two others assailed the fallen and apparently helpless pyramid-ship. They cut into its air-lock door — and gagged at the smell within. It was a living-thing smell.

It was, in fact, the personal smell of the aliens. It was inde-scribable and revolting. In all probability the aliens themselves were unconscious of it, as humans are unaware of the human smell which is so comforting to a dog. But this reek filled men with rage.

They went through the monstrous ship, hand-flashes flick-ering here and there. They were armed with nothing more deadly than spanners but they looked fiercely to see if any-thing remained alive. They ignored machinery and weapons and technical devices, seeking only dangerous life. They found none though there were many bodies.

They clambered out again and found the vehicle they'd used as a beam-mount and trundled it to the *Stellaris'* air-lock door. They helped heave off the block of plastic which acted as a giant vacuum tube.

Joe the electrician observed casually, "Say! When we were fussin' around that pyramid we musta stepped on somethin'. Their little booby-trap got all hotted up and melted itself down. Okay?"

"Very much so," Rod told him. "They'll think somebody opened it, or maybe that it went off of itself. But they won't see where we cut it open. It should puzzle them a bit. Come along!"

With two others he set the little vehicle off at top speed through the dead city's streets. His spine was literally crawling with apprehension but he went on grimly. If the newly-come fleet simply surrounded the planet and at a signal blasted it with the deadly push-pull radiation, every square inch of the planet's surface would become death itself. Nothing could live. It could happen at any instant.

And there was no conceivable defense against it.

But he'd lost twelve hours, waiting in other-space out of apprehension, overestimating the pyramid-ships' means of defense. Now he knew that a race so careful of its own life that it practised murder as a trade would be a very fearful one. It was likely to overestimate the enemy that had struck at it.

Instead of a manned ship it would probably send a robot — a drone — to investigate the weapons used against its vanquished ships. If the drone itself were destroyed the fleet would withdraw until some counter to the new weapon could be devised.

But Rod had no new weapon. He had only — he believed — the instrument by which the aliens did their murders. Even that needed to be powered by apparatus of their construction. He could not destroy anything now. So the aliens would find nothing in particular to alarm them, though it would be some time before they felt safe in landing.

Still, they could be examining the surface of the planet with telescopes — perhaps electron-telescopes — and they might detect the *Stellaris*. On the other hand they'd have to use infra-red on the night side of the planet and infra-red does not give good definition. The ship and its tiny landing-party might — might! — be safe until more light came with the dawn.

He had to risk it. He drove to the power-station. The four men cut free the isotopic dynamo and manhandled it to the vehicle. They loaded up four television-machines. They went racing back. The other load had been carried in through the air-lock. Now this load was put on board the *Stellaris*.

"I'd like to have more food," said Rod, "but we can go on short rations for awhile. All right? Seal her up!"

He took post in the control-room. Joe had connected up more switches, but there were still no instruments. He released the anchoring tractor-beams and pushed the ship up on pressors. He maneuvered above the tumbled pyramid-ship. He sent down tractors and locked them.

The *Stellaris* sank as the strain came on, but he fed more power to the pressor-beams which held up the earth-ship on unsubstantial stilt-like legs. Presently the pyramid-ship stirred and floated free. Then Rod maneuvered it very gently up against the *Stellaris'* bottom-plates and pushed up to five thousand feet.

For long minutes the ship hung there, swaying and oscillating with a soggy, burdened motion. But Rod had more controls to set by hand, since the ship was not one-tenth wired for navigation. There had to be tractors — unfocused — set to overlap in a globe all around. The force-field generators had to have certain constants changed.

That was really the ticklish part. Rod had designed the generators but he sweated as he worked. And as the crucial instant drew near he felt a despairing certainty that, from somewhere in the star-studded vault overhead, a death-beam would strike down just before he took his final action.

But it didn't.

When he raced to the control-room and glanced out the ports he saw a shimmering, faintly luminous horizon all about and many stars above. He saw far-distant darkness, which was this world's jungle, and at one place a sea.

But directly under the *Stellaris* a huge flat plate of polished metal shut off all sight of the ground. It was the pyramid-ship. Rod threw the master tractor-switch and, as the ship lurched violently, he threw the force-field switch hard over.

It was all familiar, now. There was only blackness outside and there was no weight whatever, but there were new strange grinding noises. They were against the earth-ship's hull. They were rhythmic and reverberating.

"We made it," Rod told Kit, swallowing. "I was almost sure we wouldn't have time."

Kit held fast to a hand-rail to keep from floating free.

"What's that grinding?" she asked Rod in a frightened voice.

"That's our friend, the enemy," he said. "The force-field generators were intended only to drop the *Stellaris* into other-space but I designed them so they could be changed. And I just changed them.

"I had them spread out to make a spherical field a half-mile across — well beyond our hull. So when they went on, they dropped the pyramid-ship and everything else within a quarter-mile into other-space with us."

Kit frowned bewilderedly.

"But can we *do* anything with it?" she asked. "There's no air outside and we've certainly nothing like a space-suit."

Rod grinned a little, as he wiped sweat off his forehead. "We brought air with us."

Joe the electrician came floating seraphically into the control-room.

"Near as I can figure," he reported, "we got five-six hundred feet of extension cable we can hook together to get light in that ship those critters ain't usin' any longer."

"But —" Kit grew more uneasy.

"We brought a half-mile sphere of air with us," Rod repeated. "And we've got tractors pulling in every direction. They act the same as gravity. There's a vacuum outside, of course, but there's a vacuum outside of every planet.

"Gravity holds air to the planets. Tractors are holding air to us. We can walk around on the outside of the ship if we want to. We couldn't even fall off! The tractors would pull us back, as they pull back the air."

With Joe he went to the air-lock. He cracked the door. No hiss of escaping air followed. He opened it wider. There was air outside. The *Stellaris* and its captive were in effect a miniature planet, holding an atmosphere against the emptiness of space by means of tractor-beams.

"But we've got to work fast," Rod said grimly. "I wish we

had warm clothes. This air will be losing heat to space and there's no sun to put it back. We'll be lucky to have an hour. Let's go!"

Carrying a line, with Joe uncoiling flexible light-extension wire behind him, Rod stepped out of the lock. A huge, glaring bulb glowed on the end of the wire. The tractors held them fast against the *Stellaris'* outer skin. There was the one fierce electric-light in an entire dark universe.

One tiny spot of illumination in hundreds of thousands of light-years — it showed the brightly-polished flat plating of the alien ship. A painter poked his head out of the air-lock and shivered, then gingerly followed. An arc-welder came too, carrying the tools of his trade.

They cut through the skin of the other ship, since the air-lock was no longer convenient. They pulled away masses of insulation. They cut through another skin. The repugnant reek of the pyramid-people filled their nostrils.

"We'll try to turn on their lights," observed Rod. "They must've had them! And then we start to loot the looters. Joe and I will hunt for technical stuff. The rest of you send back tools, anything that looks like books or fabrics — anything that could be interesting or useful. And work fast!"

Joe strung lights and hunted for a way to turn on the obvious sources of illumination in the first compartment they had reached. The lights remained obstinately off. Joe cut one loose and turned it over to be sent back to the *Stellaris*. Rod went on to more important matters.

The ship was amazing — not because of its development but because of its crudity. Its pyramidal form had doubtless been chosen long since because of its rigidity and because reflecting surfaces at specific angles had advantages when it was desired to go — say — near a sun.

But the ship was not the work of a really civilized race. There was no trace of artistry anywhere — not even the clean smooth lines of purely functional design. This ship looked as if it had been designed by a construction man who thought only of how to put it together. Everything else had been ignored.

It was a job that ignorant or unskilled labor could assemble and there was no particular thought for the comfort of its crew or the psychological effect of good design. The dead members of the crew were not prepossessing. Their faces were almost without features and were wholly without expression. They seemed fit occupants of a vessel designed for strict utility and nothing else.

Rod gained an increasingly strong impression that this was a case of a barbarous race suddenly acquiring a weapon they were not prepared to use except as barbarians. It appeared that just as mathematics was thousands of years ahead of technology in ancient Greece, this race had suddenly developed a specific technology thousands of years ahead of every other part of their civilization.

Used as they had used it, such an advantage would almost or quite stop progress in every other line. They would not develop a civilization of their own as long as they looted other civilizations.

He looked at the ship's weapons. He found only the push-pull beam and he'd designed it better than they had. The engine-room was absurdly simple and utterly cryptic but even there he saw clumsiness in such items as the grouping of bus-bars.

The source of power, though, did baffle him. All bus-bars ran from a triple plate of glass or plastic which had two metal plates between its leaves. It looked like a primitive condenser but apparently it supplied all the power that was used in the ship.

It was dead, now. There was no potential across it but there could be no other reading of its function than that of power-supply.

Rod had it cut loose and sent it to the *Stellaris*.

The drive was equally crude and equally improbable, until he looked at it twice. Then he held his head. It was simply a pressor-beam fined down to a needle-point and aimed at an infinitesimal hole in a metal plate.

The pressor-beam would exert a pressure of hundreds of thousands of tons upon the center of an opening only thousandths of an inch in diameter. There was a not particularly good gas-flow regulator which governed the flow of a tiny trickle of gas to the opening.

"My sainted aunt!" said Rod bitterly. "Look at it! We could have had space-travel this past fifty years! Interplanetary travel, at any rate! They let gas flow to the pin-hole and push it through with a pressor-beam! It's a pressor-beam rocket!

"Millions or billions of tons to the square inch pressure on the escaping gas! They'll get jet-velocities close to light-speed! Get this to the *Stellaris*, Joe. We'll use it, though I'm going to be ashamed. But they get more than light-speed in their ships, Joe! How'd they do that?"

He went prowling. He found the self-acting signal-device which sent a thunderous message of despair when the ship went out of action. Simple enough, save for the apparatus which used up the energy. He could not guess at the type of radiation which was produced. But nine-tenths of the things he saw were behind comparable human devices.

Men could do much better with every contrivance he understood and he suspected they could do better with the rest. This race had been enough ahead of the races it had murdered never to have to extend itself. So there was a flavor to the entire culture. It was barbarous and unpleasant and crude and revolting. It figuratively stank as its possessions did literally.

Joe the electrician tried to draw his attention. He waved him away. Other men spoke to him and he paid no heed. He searched feverishly.

The light-guns were simple. Men could make them. He found something that was obviously a type of radar. There was a vision-screen of sorts. But he hunted desperately and in vain for star-maps and for navigation-instruments.

The nearest thing he found to them was a chest from which a fierce heat still poured and which was a chaos of melted and churned-up metal and charred stuff like paper. Nothing could be made of it. It might be — it could be — that all star-maps and navigational data was automatically destroyed when the signal of despair was sent off by a shattered ship. If so, it was still more proof of the murderer-psychology of the race.

Then Kit shook his elbow insistently. Her face was white and pinched.

"You've been here two hours, Rod! It's cold! The moisture's all frozen out of the air outside the ship. The tractors pulled it down as snow! Now the air's lost so much heat it's apt to freeze too!"

Rod said harshly, "You should have stayed on the *Stellaris!* Why'd you come?"

"You wouldn't listen to anybody else!" said Kit desperately. "They said you pushed them away and kept on hunting like a crazy man! When the air freezes you can't live!"

He stared at her. Her breath was a white steam. She shivered violently. There was already a thin layer of frost on her clothes.

"All right," he said sullenly," but I want to know —"

Angrily — angry at his own incomprehension — he led her back to the opening in the pyramid-ship. There was every seeming of gravity here, created by the tractors which held an atmosphere.

Rod stepped out on the *Stellaris'* skin and there were feet of feathery snow on it. It was unbelievably cold. There was no heat in the dark universe and its emptiness sucked greedily at heat in objects from a living cosmos.

Joe stamped and chattered in the air-lock. When Rod handed Kit in he cut the cable that had furnished light in the alien ship.

"W-we got more cable from them," he gasped, "an' we got to close this lock! I'm glad I ain't a brass monkey or this cold'd ha' done me dirt!"

The outer airlock door closed. The inner one opened. There was warmth and light, and a slight pervading taint in the air from the objects the aliens had owned.

CHAPTER NINE

War Basis

FIVE minutes later Rod grimly cut off the tractors which had held an atmosphere in mid-space and an enemy space-ship with it. He found sardonic amusement in picturing the effect of that gesture upon the pyramid-folk.

The *Stellaris* still had a beam locked on the planet of the dead cities. Its power was low, but she would not be too many millions of miles away if she went back to normal space now. And the air she'd brought into the dark universe would return to normal space immediately it expanded beyond the force-fields.

There would be a sudden, violent, astounding irruption of vapor in emptiness, somewhere in sight of the planet. And a comet's tail can contain no more than a mere few cubic inches of gas, which yet is expanded and ionized and visible as a trail of hundreds of thousands of miles.

A half-mile sphere of air, expanded suddenly, should make such a sight as the stick-men had never seen before. It should fill them with enormous apprehension, simply because of its strangeness and because it followed closely on the destruction of at least three of their ships.

If they investigated and found the gutted pyramid-ship, which should go back to a star-filled cosmos somewhere near the air-cloud, they should be more uneasy still. Because they'd find their ship looted only of sample objects rather than of all its contents, and they'd realized that it had been flung contemptuously away as worthless.

But there was that loot to examine. It was more than ever unfortunate that the *Stellaris* had no gravity. The booty floated about irritatingly and those who tried to explore its possibilities floated too.

The primitive-seeming condenser remained inscrutable, though its power-leads had surely carried an enormous load. The sample light, however, glowed brightly when connected to the *Stellaris'* power-lines. But Rod was scornful.

"Mercury-vapor," he said contemptuously, "with a phosphor in the tube around it! We stopped using that sort of thing fifty years ago!"

The drive was again irritating. To all intents and purposes it was a rocket with a jet-speed astronomically high because a pressure-beam was used on it. The light-guns could have been made on Earth. The radar set had elements of novelty but Joe and Rod agreed that men made better ones. The vision-screen was not nearly as good as the ones in the dead city. Rod pushed himself away from all of them.

"They had a drive and a push-pull beam, both of which were quite within our reach," he said sourly. "Their power-supply is over my head and undoubtedly they had some trick for faster-than-light travel. But that's all! In two months we could wipe them out, given this stuff back on Earth! Since we can't get back to Earth we've got to do what we can right here!"

The other things taken from the ship, being non-technical, seemed less important. But there were bales of soft, lustrous fabric, which the girls of the air-plant oh'd and ah'd over. There were chests of prismatically glistening ware of unfamiliar shape — household luxuries of some sort and possibly tableware.

There were jewels. There were art-objects portraying flowers of exquisite delicacy and people — at least, they wore garments — which were neither the people of the planet of the yellow sun nor pyramid-folk nor any other known race.

"Those fiends didn't make this stuff," said Rod grimly. "This must come from the cities of some other poor devils they've wiped out!"

The faint taint of alien smell made his hackles tend to rise. There could never have been friendship between human beings and the people of the pyramid race under the happiest of auspices. This smell made enmity inevitable.

"We'll get to work," said Rod distastefully. "I hate to use a trick of theirs — but we need that drive."

Groping with tractor and pressor-beams was not the most efficient form of space-travel, so the alien drive was to be installed. It was simple enough to float it to a stern-ward position and weld it in place.

It needed a tiny opening for the ejected gas-particles to escape from but their speed would be so great that they'd bore their own exit. It was not so easy to weld braces and a mounting to take up its thrust. Rod left two welders swearing at the difficulty of working when they had no weight.

Kit smiled at him wrily. "Somebody has to take care of you," she said defensively when she saw him frowning. "And you'd have stayed there until you froze! I had to come after you!"

"Thanks," he said heavily. "I'm just worried because there was some stuff on that ship I didn't get. Most of their gadgets were primitive and we can do much better. But —"

"Did you find out how they got their artificial gravity?" she asked hopefully. "I get awfully tired of just floating."

"They didn't have gravity," he protested.

"But I could walk in that ship," she insisted. "I did!"

"That was our —" Rod groaned. "I'm stupid! I'll be back!"

He went to the engine-room. He pulled Joe off the drive-installation and together they set up a tractor in the extreme stern-most compartment of the ship. They widened out its beam. In less than twenty minutes objects and persons within the *Stellaris* began to settle gently toward the stern.

Thirty seconds later they had perceptible weight and after a minute weight was practically normal everywhere in the ship. Rod climbed then — though the ship was in other-space — back to face Kit in the control-room.

"We could have had gravity all along," he told her ruefully. "I only had to put a tractor in the ship's tail to pull us all toward it. Joe's setting up a pressor in the bow to neutralize it outside. So we've got gravity. Now what?"

"Nothing," said Kit wistfully, "except that it would be nice to stop worrying and think about ourselves sometimes."

"I believe," Rod told her, "there's an outside chance even of that!"

He inspected the small tractor locked on the planet of dead cities. Locked as it was, its mount adjusted its focus to allow for varying distance and it was possible to estimate the distance from the planet to the spot at which the *Stellaris* would return to normal space. It was too close. He put power on the pressor. Joe came in, uncoiling a power-lead.

"The jet drive," he said crisply. "You got a switch you ain't usin'?" He connected the cable and scrupulously labeled the switch.

"Joe," said Rod. "Remember your idea of a push-pull beam that would shoot back if we were beamed? Listen!"

He spoke carefully. Joe grinned.

"Sure! I'll fix it. Too bad we ain't got more stuff to work with."

"You might use that isotopic generator we got from the city," Rod suggested. "We can hardly run a cable out."

"Mmmm," said Joe. "It'd be a kinda good idea to try out that power-gadget from the pyramid. I got an idea about that. There's nothin' there to supply power. Nothin's used up. Nothin's breakin' down. Nothin' to happen. But it gave 'em power — in regular space."

"It's dead now." Then Rod stopped. "You think it could be a trick receiver of power from somewhere?"

"That's my hunch," said Joe. "Maybe they got broadcast power."

"Galaxy-wide?" demanded Rod skeptically. "How?"

"You guess," said Joe grinning. "I bet it's a simple trick, though — like their drive."

He nodded and went back toward the engine-room. Rod looked at his watch. There was gravity on the ship now and they had at least twice the power they'd started out with. They knew how to make weapons at least equal to any the alien pyramid-folk possessed. He remembered the pencil-beam of heat the looters had used to cut out a wall in the dead city. He'd have to look into that too. Joe was busy. His job would take time.

Rod hunted in the loot for a pencil-beam gun and found one. On the way back he stopped to watch Joe at work on the automatic push-pull weapon. Joe had only such tools as had been on the ship during its construction but he was doing a good job. Rod watched approvingly.

"Joe," he said after a moment, "if you sliced that tensor-plate into segments and fixed the feedback so —"

He illustrated.

"If you do that," Rod finished, "it will shoot back only in the direction from which it's shot at. All the power'll go into a relatively narrow beam." Then another idea struck him.

"My sainted aunt! Better than that, Joe, set the feed-back

like this! There's no pull on a tractor until it hits something. When there's a tractor going out from every segment — better put a commutator on and run through them in turn — when there's a tractor going out and it hits something, that will turn on the push-pull beam! Full-power too!"

Joe grunted. He looked at Rod with a wry expression.

"It's a bright idea all right. We're turnin' the old *Stellaris* into a warship, sure enough. But we won't be good company for nice people. We're goin' to go roamin' around like a mad dog?"

"A shunt here will take care of that," said Rod. "With the shunt cut in it will ring a bell when a tractor-beam hits. With a power-switch in parallel we can make it shoot back and then tell us what it did."

Joe looked relieved. "Y-yeah. I see that." He grinned twistily. "I'd hate to go around spittin' death-beams just automatic. We'd wind up kinda lonesome, seems like."

Rod went back to the control-room. But the weapon that was developing stayed in his mind. He went back again and asked Joe to make an adjustment so the push-pull power-feed could be cut off from any desired segment, so that one part of the weapon's range could be left unblasted if desired.

"I'm acting," he said, almost embarrassed, "as if I thought we might find friends."

Joe grunted. "Well? Those guys in the pyramid-ships are tough babies. Maybe the folks they killed were good guys. There's usually a good guy somewhere to make up for a bad one."

Then he added, "I'll have this thing ready in a coupla hours. You know how we're goin' to mount it outside? No air there now!"

Rod sketched out a notion for that too. Joe grunted again.

"That's half an hour more. I'll set those welder-guys workin' on it."

Back to the control-room again. Rod paced up and down, no longer really conscious of the novelty of gravity in space. The ship began to feel like something other than a hulk navigated by makeshift means.

He began to feel less like a shipwreck victim and more like a man in command of a ship. He began, indeed, to think in terms of what could be done to the pyramid-race, instead of the peril they represented.

It was nearer three hours than two before Joe reported the new weapon finished. It had called for very careful work by practically every man on the ship and the using up of I-beams intended for interior partitions.

When it was complete, Rod threw the switch that meant a return to normal space. There was practically no change in sensation as dots of light appeared in the vision-ports and ran through all the colors of the rainbow before they settled to their usual appearance as stars by myriads on every hand. The yellow sun was now very far away. It was only the brightest distant object in the heavens.

They opened the airlock door, with a tractor covering the opening so no air would escape. Focused pressors pushed the new device outside and maneuvered it delicately to a new position. From the ports Rod guided it to the *Stellaris'* nose and anchored it. And then a tiny tractor pulled back the switch that set the generator into action and the *Stellaris* was a fighting ship.

For the first time Rod applied the jet-drive. The ship gave a mighty surge forward.

It headed for the yellow star — and battle.

CHAPTER TEN

Battle!

THEY had seen four planets on their first approach to this solar system. One a world all ice from pole to pole, they had by-passed for the next world sunward. There were two others still nearer to the sun. Rod regarded them speculatively as the *Stellaris* drove toward the world of dead cities.

"I think," he said meditatively, "that I'm going to take a look at those planets — if we live through this."

Kit stood beside him.

"And somehow that settles it. Do you realize, Rod, how completely you are expected to decide things? One of the painters said we should be trying to find our own sun or else hunting a planet we can settle on. But Joe said he was crazy and there wasn't even an argument. You wanted to fight, so there simply wasn't any question about it."

"There's a reason for us to fight," said Rod curtly. "Nobody can guess the size of the pyramid-ship fleet but it's surely all hunting us. If we stay in one place, fighting, maybe they'll think we're survivors of the race they murdered.

"We have to try to make them think so for the sake of Earth. If they decided they'd better start a general massacre of all the races we could come from, Earth would certainly be included. And there's no faintest preparation to stop them back there."

Joe came climbing up from the engine-room. "That thing that looks like a condenser," he reported amiably, "it works. It's hot now — plenty of power. I hooked it up an' we're runnin' on it."

"Then unhook it," commanded Rod sharply. "Get back to our own power! That doesn't work in the dark universe and we couldn't go into it or stay in it! Shift the leads back! *Quick!*"

Joe's mouth dropped open. He dived for the engine-room again. Rod's forehead creased. Minutes later Joe came back, crestfallen.

"Sorry," he said apologetically. "I thought it was kinda humorous to use their own power to fight 'em with. We're back on our own now."

"It's broadcast power, all right," said Rod grimly. "Somehow they can fill the whole Galaxy with power for their ships to draw on — unless they've found a source of energy that comes from nothingness itself."

After a moment he added, "I keep thinking about those inner planets. It's a hunch. It bothers me. It doesn't seem quite natural." He shook his head as if to clear it. "Those devils must have broadcast power of some sort, though."

A bell rang sharply. It stopped. It rang again. It stopped. It rang again. Rod and Joe tensed.

"What does that mean?" asked Kit apprehensively.

"It should mean that we blasted a pyramid-ship," Rod told her. "This is a long way out, though."

The sun was again a glaring disk. Something winked in its rays. It vanished. It winked again out a right-hand port. It was infinitely small and the effect was that of a bit of tinsel spinning in a bright light.

"Right!" said Rod in satisfaction. "A pyramid-ship sentry. Our beam-gun on the bow found him and blasted him, probably before he knew anything about it. His skipper probably had a spasm as he died and jammed his controls, so he's spinning."

The bell rang on monotonously, once in each revolution of the commutator which applied full power to each segment of the tensor-plate in turn, to blast any target the device might find. The pyramid-ship was getting a fresh lethal dose of the push-pull beam at each clang of the bell.

Onward the *Stellaris* bored. Presently the bell stopped.

Rod said, "Hm — we left him behind. We've got to allow for that! We can't have them coming up behind us, where the ship fills up a space and the beams turned off."

"Will we beam the planets, Rod?" asked Kit.

"We've got a minus arrangement," Rod told her. "We don't shoot at anything over a certain range. I don't know exactly what it is but it's probably some thousands of miles."

The planet of the dead race was a perceptible disk now. It was the size of a pea. Time passed. It grew to the size of a marble.

The bell rang. Twice. It stopped and rang twice again — and again — and again.

"Two more of them," said Rod savagely.

Time passed. The double-ring stopped. There was silence. Then a single ring again, monotonously repeated.

"This ain't sportin'," said Joe, scowling, "but y'don't play sportin' with rats."

The planet was the size of a peach, now. There was an infinitesimal shimmering in space ahead — an infinitely thin sliver of what looked like gossamer came up out of the planet's atmosphere. It spread and formed itself into a geometric pattern of wavering specks of light.

"They know we knocked off their ships," said Rod. He was thinking aloud. "They've plenty of sentries out and when a ship dies, it squeals to the rest. Automatically. So they know we can hit, and hard. But they're forming up to fight us. How'll they fight?"

The *Stellaris* sped furiously toward the enemy formation. There was silence. Then Kit gasped.

"Rod, I feel queer — like that other ti —"

Rod's hands moved like lightning. The force-field switch crashed over. He said distinctly — with the ports all black — "The rats!"

They were in the dark universe for a bare second. He flung

the switch back once more. There was no difference in the feel of things now, whether in other-space or normal. The *Stellaris* had dodged only momentarily into the other set of dimensions but in the other-space her velocity was enormous.

Rod, however, overestimated it. He had thought the *Stellaris* would slip back into the universe of stars beyond the enemy fleet. But she winked into being in its very midst.

There were shining pyramidal shapes on every hand. The bell burst into frenzied, continuous clanging. Glittering metal ships flashed past the ports so swiftly that the eye could not focus on them.

But the *Stellaris'* weapon poured out death — the death of the pyramid-folk's own contriving — as the Earth-ship hurtled through the fleet of space-murderers and went on beyond them. She was through before they could train a single weapon.

Then Rod swung her about to face the enemy. The drive-jet fought her acquired momentum. The ship slowed — and kept its beam-weapon going as it struggled to dash in again.

Minute by minute the clanging of the bell grew less. Despite her drive the ship was only slowing. She had not stopped. But when the planet's disk ceased to recede and began to grow visibly larger once more—when her savage second charge was evident — Rod saw flickerings as pyramid-ships deserted their formation and fled toward emptiness.

The main body of the fleet did not disperse. It did not flee. But as minute after minute passed, it became apparent that something was wrong. The edges of the pyramid-formation grew fuzzy. The ships did not keep station.

When the *Stellaris* bored into them again the bell clanged and clanged and clanged. At the thickest part of the fleet it rang frantically, one sharp stroke for each outpouring of the push-pull beam at an individual target. But the ships made no concerted move, nor any purposeful individual ones. The *Stellaris* was merely killing again ships that were already dead.

Minutes more and she was through a second time and the first space-battle in all the history of the galaxy was over. One Earth-ship that had taken off from its home planet by pure accident, unarmed and unequipped, had wiped out nine-tenths of a fleet that had never before been opposed. And its remnants were in flight.

The *Stellaris* drove on and on. The unmanned hulks which had been fighting vessels only a little while since fell astern. The clamor of the bell lessened. Presently there were only random disconnected sounds.

Later there were none at all.

"Not too nervy," commented Rod. "They saw we had them licked and those that were left headed for home. It fits the way their minds seem to work."

"What will we do now?" asked Kit. "Land on the planet again?"

Rod considered, scowling. "Part of the fleet ran away as soon as they found their broadside was no good."

"Broadside?"

"Massed push-pull beams," said Rod shortly. "They turned the beams of the whole fleet on us. We shouldn't have been able to live through it to get within range with a single ship's weapons. Probably wouldn't, at that, only you felt queer.

"That was the first-aligned beams hitting us, away out of range for a few beams but well in range for the bunch of them! Another second and that blast would have been so strong nothing in creation could have stood it. Certainly we couldn't!" He paused.

"Some of them, though, ran from a fleet action. They're not a very brave race. I'm trying to figure something out. The ships on the ground knew we'd knocked off their sentries. Of course! So we were dangerous.

"So maybe some of them didn't take off with the rest of the fleet. Playing it safe. It would seem to fit in with the way their minds work. So maybe some ships are still skulking on the ground."

"So?" Kit waited.

"If we can spot them they're dead ducks. But if we tried to land they might knock us down practically from ambush. They're probably half shivering in deadly fear and half licking their chops as they wait for us to land. So —"

He looked abruptly at Kit, and then at Joe. Joe grinned.

"I guess we stop off at one of those other planets?"

"That'll be it," said Kit confidently.

Rod's eyes narrowed, even as he released the small hand-tractor which kept the deadly contrivance on the ship's bow in action.

"Ye-e-e-s," he said slowly. "I guess that will be it. We'll see what is to be seen. But I think I'm going to be mighty cagey!"

He swung the *Stellaris* about on her course.

The line of flight of a space-ship is not at all the same thing as — say — the path of a ground-vehicle. When a ground vehicle, moving south, turns east it travels east and stops moving south. A space-ship doesn't. The space-ship doesn't stop moving south. There's nothing to stop it.

When a course is changed the new line of movement simply modifies the one the ship followed before and that is the result of all its previous courses. A southward-moving space-ship which heads east actually travels on a line somewhere between south and east.

The exact line depends on the acceleration of the ship, how long it was on the southerly course, and how long it continues on the eastern one. Its direction of motion changes with each of those factors. So that to sight for a planet from space, as the *Stellaris* did, and then head for it, is no way to reach it.

Rod probably knew it in theory but he realized it the hard way. The yellow sun's second planet had a proper motion all its own, which Rod did not know. The *Stellaris* had a motion all its own, which was the result of all the courses it had followed during two full days in two different universes. But nevertheless, Rod aimed the ship at the second planet and drove for it.

Hours passed and the *Stellaris* was farther from the planet than when it started. More, it no longer pointed at the planet though the distant stars it aimed at were the same. Rod tried again and the same thing happened. In the end, scowling, he swung a tractor on the elusive world, waited an astonishing four full minutes for the beam to take hold and then grumpily set Joe on watch and went to sleep. It was his second period of rest in more clock-days than he could count up.

He slept heavily for a long, long time. He waked and Kit brought him food. It was strictly vegetable and vaguely unsatisfying. He ate, only half-awake, and went back to sleep again.

This time he dreamed. And oddly, it was not a dream of Earth or of the battle just past or even of Kit, whom he could not allow to absorb him too much in the present state of things. He dreamed of the dead race on the yellow sun's planet — the race which was now only a multitude of crumpled heaps of brightly-colored garments.

In his dream he saw a space-ship rise from the third planet and land upon another. He dreamed of a tiny colony established there before this space-ship made its flight. This ship landed on a hitherto unexplored part of this new planet and the colonists just moving to the new planet found a vague metal object there.

They meddled with it and immediately they died — not only the meddlers, but those in the grounded space-ship nearby. And then the object melted itself to a mere pool of bubbling metal, which was found by members of the already-established colony much, much later.

The space-ship itself was smashed as if by explosives. And

after that there was no more communication between the colony on this other world and the planet from which they had come. The colonists simply lived on, bewildered and helpless.

As a dream it was at once remarkable and suspicious. It was reasonable enough as a rationalization of a hunch. But Rod wondered cagily why his subconscious had pictured no metal pyramid as the object the colonists-to-be had meddled with? Why not a pyramid with sculptured figures on its sides?

It was a very vivid dream. Of course he'd been thinking of other races endangered by the pyramid-ships. Joe had said something about good guys existing to make up for the bad ones. And he'd thought unreasonably often of the yellow sun's second planet. Especially lately. Even when his mind should have been full of battle-plans as the *Stellaris* sped toward a fight.

It could be a hunch, of course. He'd had a hunch before — on the dead planet, when he was making a push-pull beam to wipe out the looters there. He'd felt deadly danger without knowing why he felt it.

He'd worked frantically, racing against time, though he knew of no real reason why he should fear the coming of looters to the city the *Stellaris* had landed in. And that hunch and the hurry it caused had saved him and Joe and a painter then and there and probably the *Stellaris* besides.

The hunch and the dream and the constant thought of the second planet fitted together a little too well. It was plausible that uneasiness should show up as a hunch. It was reasonable enough that an urge to visit a planet should show up in a dream as a concocted explanation of a reason why he should go there. But he didn't believe it.

The real cause of his dream didn't know that the killer-race made its booby-traps in the form of pyramids. The real cause of his dream didn't picture a pyramid on the second planet, though almost certainly one had been there to cause the murder of a race.

Rod got up, thinking coldly. He heard Joe's voice, angry.

"That ring-tailed haystack ain't goin' to lick us! If we set out to hit some place we're goin' to hit it."

Rod stepped into the control-room. Kit was there, looking anxiously ahead.

Joe shook his fist at a forward vision-port.

"Morning," said Rod, drily. "I must've slept the clock around. What's up?"

Then he saw. The second planet loomed large and very near. It appeared to be merely a featureless fleecy white. That would be clouds. But on closer view the clouds were not wholly solid.

They were in masses which sometimes merely thinned at their junctures, and sometimes separated a little to show a darkness below them, the whole producing a mottled semi-marble effect. But the *Stellaris* was not approaching the planet. It rotated serenely at a seemingly fixed distance.

"We been tryin' to get down onto that hunka cussedness yonder," explained Joe, indignantly. "But the closer we come the quicker it dodges! We been clean around it a dozen times already an' we can't get a bit closer! What're they doin' down there? Pushin' us off with a pressor?"

Rod grinned. He thought he understood the dream now.

"Hardly! We've got a lateral velocity and we're hung tight to the planet by a tractor beam. So we're in an orbit around it. Naturally we can't get down like that!"

"Says who?" demanded Joe pugnaciously, scowling at the planet.

"Says me," Rod told him. "We'll get down through." He took over what controls there were. "When I was a kid I used to twirl a weight on a string and get it going fast, then let it wind itself up on my finger. Did you?"

"Uh-huh, but what's that got to do with this?" demanded Joe.

"It's the trick," said Rod. "As the string wound up and got shorter, the weight went around faster and faster. Remember? But it didn't go faster in feet per second, just twirls per second. That's us. The closer we get the faster we go around it — and our tractor-beam will stretch. That's all. I'll fix it."

He swung the ship until the fleecy planet was straight abeam. He put on full drive in the direction opposite that of the planet's seeming motion.

"How long do we take to get around?" he asked.

"Less'n an hour," said Joe angrily. "You can tell. There's one place where it looks like a mountain or something sticks up through the clouds."

Rod nodded. That checked. "We'll land there."

He watched. The *Stellaris'* drive produced no visible effect for a long time and it seemed insane to try to descend to a planet's surface by driving at right-angles to the desired descent. But that was the only way it could be done.

Presently the passage of the mottled misty surface seemed slower. At the very farthest edge of the visible hemisphere, a speck of solidity appeared. Rod stepped up the drive again.

Then the mottlings were visibly larger. As the planet seemed to slow, the mottlings continued to increase in size.

"We're coming close, now," said Rod. "We'll be holding off on pressors, presently."

It was true. The sphere beneath slowed to a snail's pace and it was very near indeed. The speck of solidity vanished and reappeared, and vanished and reappeared. Mist sometimes boiled over it, sometimes left it in plain view.

Rod began to juggle tractor and pressor-beams. He adjusted the jet-drive. At long last the planet's surface seemed stationary and he cut off the jet. He began, very carefully, to let the ship down into atmosphere.

"I'm going to make a guess," he said meditatively. "When we get down to that mountain-tip — it's the only one that pierces the clouds — we'll find a big mass of stuff that once was melted metal. And not too far away we'll find a smashed-up space-ship. Not a pyramid-ship, this one, but a ship made back on the planet that's dead now."

Kit looked at him, and her mouth opened. Then the logic of the statement appeared.

"I think I see," she said slowly. "You mean it would have been easier for the people of the dead cities to reach this planet than the snow-covered one because it comes nearer. And the one place where solid ground shows would be the place where a space-ship would land. Also it would be the one place where the pyramid-people would have put something to tell them when it was touched."

Rod grimaced. "I spoke too sensibly," he said. "Now I'll make a prophecy. When we land we'll wait. And presently some survivors of the race of the next planet out will come to us. And I think they'll be friendly."

Joe blinked. "Ghosts?"

"No. Real people," Rod assured him. "People that happened not to be home when their world was murdered but perfectly real people. You saw what they were like in the televisors."

"How'll they come?" demanded Joe skeptically. "Space-ships?"

"More likely aeroplanes," said Rod, working the ship down with infinite pains. "Maybe ground-vehicles. But they'll come!"

In this, though, he was wrong. He let down the *Stellaris* with the utmost of painstaking care. There was air outside, and winds. There was a vast sea of cloud and streamers of mist that writhed up from it.

Sometimes the mountain-top was hidden by white stuff. Sometimes it was laid bare. But at long last the *Stellaris* settled with a noticeable jolt upon the barren rock of what appeared to be an upward-slanted small plateau rather than a pointed peak.

Rod pointed out a port. There, in plain view from where the ship touched ground, was a shining, mirror-like surface. It had been a liquid once. It was solid metal now. A quarter-mile away there was a shattered carcass which was only a quarter of the *Stellaris'* size but surely had once been a nearly spherical space-ship.

But Rod was mistaken about waiting, about having people of the supposedly dead race come to them.

They didn't have to wait. The people were already there on the mountain-top, waiting for them.

CHAPTER ELEVEN

In the Cards

THE *Stellaris* settled again through thick and swirling mists Slowly and cautiously, and slowly and cautiously, she moved down toward the white oblivion the clouds promised and produced.

There were strange people in the control-room of the Earthship. The tallest was no more than four and a half feet tall and they were distinctly rotund, all of them. They made clear high-pitched sounds to each other, and now and again one of them put urgent hands upon Rod at the controls and made the same clear sounds to him.

At such times the sounds made sense. When there was physical contact there was meaning in the musical tones of the small people. At other times they were only sounds — very musical, more or less pleasant, but only sounds.

But of course the same could be said of any unfamiliar Earth language.

Rod had been prepared for it. After all, he'd had a highly useful hunch in a dead city and he'd been obsessed with the thought of coming to this planet, and he'd had a dream which ignored information he possessed.

Had his own subconscious mind dictated that dream, it would surely have pictured a metal pyramid on the cloud-wreathed world as the origin of the pool of metal. But the dream did not picture that at all.

When the other facts were taken into consideration it added up to limited, incomplete information from somewhere, from a source which had some knowledge that Rod did not possess and lacked some data that he did.

Explanation was complete, now. The dream was accurate as far as it went. The little people now in the ship's control-room had been very brave indeed. They'd come out of the mist to meet the *Stellaris* as it landed and they'd made gestures obviously intended as a welcome.

And Rod had gone out to them. He carried a flame-weapon taken from the captured pyramid-ship but he left it in his pocket. He had no uneasiness about the air because the small people breathed it and the air of their home planet was suitable for humans.

So the group of half a dozen rotund figures and Rod — inevitably grim — had met on the top of the one mountain to rise above the planet's clouds. There was not exactly tenseness in the air. Rod felt an anxious, an actually desperate sensation of hope and fear together, communicated to him in the odd fashion of a hunch.

He spoke. His tone was dry. "We're all in the same jam, it seems. And with a community of dislikes we ought to be friends."

Flutelike notes filled his ears. Then a short round figure approached, very hesitantly, and held out two hands. They were not human hands but they were empty. Rod put out his own. The round figure almost apologetically moved closer and very tentatively offered to touch hands with Rod.

"I'll try anything once," said Rod. "Go ahead!"

The hands touched. The round man's flesh was warm and firm. But instantly the high-pitched sounds were language. Urgent, apprehensive words. It was even reasonable that comprehension should follow physical contact but Rod did not wait for theoretic discussion. He spoke himself and his words were understood.

Minutes later he led the way to the air-lock.

"These people," he said crisply inside the ship, with the small group clustered behind him. "These people are members of a colony from the planet we visited. They know the rest of their race is wiped out. They've every reason to be our friends.

"If you hold hands with them you can talk. We'll work out explanations later. Right now we're going to shift the *Stellaris* down out of sight beneath the clouds. Get talking to them and find out all you can."

And then he went to the control-room with the rotund man who had first touched hands with him. He prepared to shift the *Stellaris*. Here, atop the mountain, at least sometimes it could be sighted from space and bathed in a deadly push-pull beam.

The ship rose on her pressor-beams. She moved. But navigation in a world of mist was ticklish. Rod had to feel his way cautiously. More, the small people had come a long way to greet the Earth-ship. It was necessary to ease the unwieldy space-craft through many passes among high and unseen mountains.

There were moments when he was absorbed in the task and the trilling speech of the little folk was a disturbance. And there were many times when warm hands touched him irritatingly — but at each such contact the twitterings became intelligible — and he received useful knowledge about his immediate problem. He was beginning to feel more tolerant.

When the mountains were cleared there was a long flight of some hundreds of miles over unseen level stuff which might have been either flat land or sea. Rod did not like it. He liked to see what he was doing. But in snatches between the more practical data on course and height he caught fragments of twittering not meant for his ears. And they were reassuring.

When at long last he set the ship down — it was actually the third time he had brought her to ground since her lunatic departure from Earth — when at long last he landed again he was reasonably satisfied about the small folk. But he was wholly dissatisfied with the picture of the future as they saw it. He was not even very much pleased with the ship's surroundings when he cut off the power.

The *Stellaris* lay in a forest of gigantic trees, with trunks from ten to fifty feet in diameter. There was everywhere a gray twilight. Huge wide-spreading branches at once shut out a view of the clouds and seemed to form a roof which kept out the mist, so that the space beneath them was clear.

Later one of the biological assistants told Kit that the order of things in vegetation was reversed in these trees. Instead of taking moisture from the ground and losing it through the leaves, these trees absorbed water through their foliage and sent it down to their roots.

But under their protection the colony from the third planet had set itself up to survive. There was a tiny power-house, quaintly like the architecture of the dead cities in its details. There were small houses. And everywhere, some fifty to a hundred feet up on the tree-trunks, there were light-projectors to throw light down on the colony and its inhabitants and their cultivated fields.

On a cloud-covered planet there would not be much ultra-violet and under such a forest there would be none at all. But lights could substitute. The colony could survive and feed itself. But it was very small. There were no more than two hundred individuals remaining of a race that had dotted a planet with cities.

When the humans emerged from the ship they could feel the overwhelming relief from tension the welcoming-party's report had brought. Rod was led at once to the colony's head. And — holding hands absurdly — they plunged into the business before them.

For the rest the establishment of friendship and understanding was the most urgent of needs. Kit took half a dozen of the little round women into the *Stellaris*. She held hands and talked and they readily understood her.

They exclaimed politely over the *Stellaris*, but it was clear that they considered its incompletion uncivilized. Only after Kit explained the accidental and unpremeditated beginning of the voyage were they quite convinced. Then they expressed engaging sympathy.

But when they saw the loot taken from the pyramid-ship — the lustrous fabrics, and the delicately prismatic plastic-ware, and the flowers and seeming people on the other art-objects — they were fascinated.

They could not understand how people who made such things could be murderers. Then Kit explained that it was apparently loot from still another murdered race and she fairly felt the burning hatred the small people knew.

When Rod came back to the ship she was full of news.

"Rod, they're adorable!" she told him enthusiastically. "They are civilized! They are charming! I've found out about telepathy, Rod. They say that telepathy's never quite satisfactory because no two people see things exactly the same way.

"A square or a circle doesn't look quite the same to me as it does to you, Rod. So there's normally a fogginess in anything like thought-transference because you're trying to see through somebody else's eyes."

Rod nodded.

"But words do help to get thoughts into a pattern that can be transmitted," Kit went on breathlessly. "And with contact real communication is possible. When they talk and hold hands they get each other's meanings much more accurately than we do.

"Outside of that they can only pick up emotions, not thoughts. They know how you feel but not what you think. And they knew that their race was dead when they couldn't pick up any feeling of the race's emotions.

"They were able to tell when the looters were on the planet because their emotions were alien and contemptuous. But when they picked up our emotions of horror and sympathy and anger at what we saw they knew we'd come and weren't the murderers!"

"I know," said Rod tiredly. "The whole colony held hands and all of them tried to warn us about the looters but all they could do was make me jumpy. Before the battle they were trying again."

"They could only make us interested in the inner planets. After I went to sleep they were able to make me dream but they can't do more than that without physical contact and it took all of them working together to do so much."

"It's wonderful that they're able to do that much," said Kit.

"Very wonderful," said Rod in some bitterness. "They brought us here with it. But do you think we can take all of them on the *Stellaris*? Will our air-purifier keep them from suffocating with us if they stay on board indefinitely?"

Kit looked blank. "I don't suppose so. It's kept the air good for us."

"Fifteen people! Add two hundred more. What then?"

"But they're all right here, aren't they?"

"For how long?" demanded Rod. "We had one brief contact with a space-ship just out of Earth. All our other contacts have been here in this solar system. The pyramid-people murdered this race because they made a space-ship and it was only luck that this colony'd been started before they learned of it. We figured that if we stayed here those fiends would think we were survivors and not guess we came from Earth. Now there *are* survivors! So what happens?"

Kit shook her head. He said savagely, "Those rats hunt for us — as a colony. They find these people — a colony. They wipe them out for what we've done! I've been talking to the colony head. There's no evading it. That's in the cards."

CHAPTER TWELVE

Boarders

SHRILL twitterings down below. The voice of Joe the electrician, just coming in the air-lock.

"Okay, fellas! If you can make anything outa it, you're welcome! Anyhow, it's plenty hot if you can use the power."

His voice died away and the twitterings with it. He was taking a group of the small round men into the engine-room, doubtless to show them the condenser-device from the pyramid-ship the *Stellaris'* crew had looted.

"If we hadn't turned up," said Rod, "those fiends would never have suspected that there were survivors. The colony could have gone on for centuries, building up a new civilization maybe and knowing about space-murderers and working out ways of fighting them when they dared take to space again. But we turned up. We've spoiled that idea!"

He spread out his hands. "Those rats will look for *us*. They'll find *them*. If we go away and leave these people here they'll be murdered like the rest of their race. Because of us! And we can't allow that!"

"N-naturally," said Kit distressedly. "Of course we can't. But what can we do?"

"That's what's got to be worked out," Rod told her grimly. "We can depend on the pyramid-ships coming back. And with an answer to our last trick, too!"

He felt something close to despair. There are obligations that cannot be evaded. If the *Stellaris* had made the race of murderers suspect the existence of a colony, where there was none, that was warfare. But to cause those murderers to search for a colony which did exist was something else. Human beings can't do that sort of thing and go off untroubled.

Joe came in, beaming. "Those little guys are pretty smart," he said contentedly. "They take that condenser that's a power-picker-up an' chirp at each other an' tell me they think they know somethin' that they can figure out that gizmo from. They say they got a hunch it's even the answer to faster-than-light travel. So they go off, cartin' it precious, to see what they see. Okay?"

Rod nodded. He sat scowling at the mass of unfilled spaces which should have been the *Stellaris'* instrument-board.

"Listen, Joe," he said heavily. "Those pyramid-rats have taken a licking. From us. But they can't leave it at that. They can't stay licked. They've committed so many crimes they can't stop. If any other race gets space travel and they can't wipe that race out the pyramid-people get wiped out. They know it. They can't make friends now. It's too late!"

Joe said amiably, "Those little guys won't make friends, that's sure! Maybe they got squeaky high voices but they know what hate is! They were asking me questions about the cities yonder an' the way I could tell they felt made my hair curl!"

Rod said impatiently, "What do you think the pyramid-ships will come back with? I doubt they're too smart. They made some discoveries and used them for weapons and apparently were satisfied to stop at that. Their ships are no more civilized than a pirate ship in the old days. But they've got to work out some way to handle us. What'll it be?"

Joe sat on the corner of what was intended for a navigator's table, if a navigator should ever acquire star-maps and navigating instruments. He swung one foot.

"What I'd do? Hm — we come out of other-space right in the middle of their fleet an' knock 'em off by dozens before they can slap a beam on us, an' we're gone, still fightin', before they come to — them that's left. If I had to cook up somethin' it'd be to handle a ship that turned up in my lap."

Rod waited, frowning.

"An' it looks to me," said Joe, "like if I thought somebody was goin' to do that I'd have beams goin' out in all directions ,as soon as I thought he was thinkin' about it. If there was any way to keep 'em from bumping off my own gang —"

Rod jumped. "Right. I keep thinking in terms of our outfitting. But they've got measuring instruments! They can calibrate their beams! They could mount push-pull generators that would kill up to ten thousand miles but not beyond.

"Then they could space their ships fifteen thousand miles apart and have a fifty-percent overlap and a formation that'd fill up the whole solar system! All such a fleet would need to do would be simply to sweep through a solar system and everything in it would be dead! If we charged a formation like that or tried to turn up in its middle . . ."

Joe nodded. "Uh-huh. We'd get a dose of push-pull beam that'd knock us off in a hurry."

"And what's more —" Rod's forehead cleared. "Since they haven't got other-space force-fields they probably think we can jump from a standing start to light-speed or better. That would seem to explain our jumping through their beam into their laps!"

Joe swung his foot, unperturbed. "Uh-huh." Then he said,

"Those little guys are pretty good with tools. How much time you think we got?"

"Not much! The ships that escaped have got to get back to base, wherever that may be. They've got to work out a new trick — which will probably be that one — and mount new projectors and calibrate them and then come back. But it won't take long!"

Joe said amiably, "A focused tractor works from the other-space to this. You think it'd work from this to the other space? An' a pressor, too?"

"Why not?" Then Red stared. "Are you thinking of a drone? That would be the trick, of course."

"Yeah," said Joe, grinning. "I'd scare the pants off 'em if they saw the ol' *Stellaris* amblin' right up to 'em through all the beams they could pour into her, wipin' 'em out copious an' not havin' a whisker curled by the worst they could do. They'd figure they were goners sure!" Then he added, "If we got time to fix it."

"That," said Rod sourly, "is the question!"

It was a very urgent question. And there were others. But answers of a sort were forthcoming for most. As for the time before a refurbished pyramid-fleet could be expected back, the small people could promise some telepathic warning.

As they'd known of their race's death by the absence of any emotions to perceive, and of the coming of looters on the planet by their scorn, and of the landing of the *Stellaris* by the much more sympathetic emotions of its occupants at sight of the murdered cities — so they could know of the space-fleet's return.

But they could not get the slightest inkling of any technical improvements in the enemy ships by their psychic gift. They simply couldn't read thoughts — only feelings.

Feverish activity commenced. The small people began to make a double of the *Stellaris* — a double in appearance only.

It was a mere shell of thin metal put over a frame that would hold it in shape. Some of their technicians began a feverish duplication of the fighting-device on the *Stellaris'* bow.

The arc-welders from the ship welded that in place and so released tractors that had anchored it. Joe ran cables into the control-room and set up something like adequate indicators — getting the needed instruments from the colony's small store.

Work went on frantically in the *Stellaris'* flotation-bulges too. There was no time to build new sections to the ship but the flotation-bulges now served no purpose.

Heavily insulated inside, with heating-elements provided, they could accommodate a great addition to the hydroponic gardens which kept the ship's air fresh. The small folk, too, had plants which would serve to excellent purpose. They would provide food in vast quantities.

The matter of food for the first time was solved. The colonists had plenty and the colony had necessarily been staffed with technologists needed for its survival. The dieticians discussed matters in great detail with the several humans. They made tests. They painstakingly experimented.

In two days from the *Stellaris'* landing, the diet of its human crew was wholly bearable. There was a close approximation of bread, and a very near similitude of three or four different vegetables — but the ones from the ship's air-rooms still tasted better.

There was even a pretty good imitation of steak, which the dietitians assured Kit contained all the needed amino-acid chains the human being required, plus the fats they had begun hungrily to crave. It was not exactly right — not exactly — but it was a great deal better than they'd had.

The real triumph, however, was in the technical department. The little round men used the same plastic "vacuum-tube" that Rod had salvaged from the planet. They had two others, which were smaller. They used the condenser-device from the pyramid-ship also for power.

The imitation *Stellaris* was an empty shell but for a complex, heavily-built device in its very center. That device did not include a drive, because there were reinforced plates on which the real *Stellaris* could focus tractor and pressor-beams, so that its pseudo-twin could be maneuvered and moved from a distance.

But in place of the drive there were tiny beams focused on devices in the *Stellaris* which performed the functions of cables. The power in those beams would vary to communicate information to the *Stellaris* even in other-space. And the little men dismantled the four televisors and set their scanners in the giant robot they were constructing. The receiving-screens went in the Earth-ship's control-room.

Altogether an incredible lot was done. The Earth-ship was no longer alone. She had a fighting-ship for companion, unmanned, to be sure, but which had at least five times the power-supply of the parent vessel and her fighting-beam was deadly.

With many hands to work on it, all inspired alike by hatred and equipped with skill, that fighting-beam was a monstrous engine for destruction.

The push-pull beams were ingeniously designed to scan all space with fifty times the rapidity of the first device and to linger briefly on any found target.

They had the power of a generator designed to supply a metropolis, plus two smaller generators intended to furnish a colony not only with ordinary power but the means of combatting a strange environment, plus a power-unit from an enemy space-ship itself. The beam of this single ship should have nearly the range of a fleet-broadcast of the enemy.

But it was, of course, a robot.

Two days passed — three — four. Then there were twitterings in all the compartments of the *Stellaris* as the round little colonists crowded into it. They carried small possessions.

They had already moved stores and highly useful supplies into the ship's unfinished storage-rooms. They were, to all intents and purposes, abandoning their colony, because their entire solar system would be blasted when the pyramid-fleet returned. And the *Stellaris* seemed crowded.

It was necessary. Twenty of the little folk had been on watch since the beginning. They sat in a circle, holding hands in a quaint absorption.

They were aware, of course, of the emotions of their fellows and of the humans around them. But they carefully ignored those sensations.

They must have felt a curious loneliness as they listened or watched — however the process could be described by which they waited for the sensations of alien presences which would tell of the return of the enemy fleet.

It was coming. It was coming fast. The air-lock was sealed. The *Stellaris* thrust up-ward on those invisible stilts which were pressor-beams and Rod drew the pseudo-ship after him as cloud-banks swirled around the Earth-ship.

He had controls for this ship, now. He swung it past the *Stellaris* as it wallowed in the impenetrable mist.

He sent the drone out of atmosphere into space.

Warm hands clasped him urgently. Twitterings.

They had meaning.

"It seems that they come faster than light. They are very triumphant. Their emotions suggest that they will slow to visibility only after they enter this system and that they will flash through it, destroying everything in an instant without any possibility of reply."

"That," said Rod with some confidence, "is what they think!"

An hour later he no longer had confidence. An hour later the *Stellaris* was beaten, its drone crippled. It fled madly through other-space while the pyramid-ship systematically wrought destruction upon all the planets of the yellow sun. If any life had remained it no longer did so.

CHAPTER THIRTEEN

Defeat

AT FIRST, it did seem that the battle would go Rod's way. The drone-ship went up into sunlit space from the the cloudy covering of the second planet. Hidden in the mist, Rod had to interpret the look of things from the television-screen in the control-room.

In a very real sense the vision-screens were superior to eyesight. There was an adjustment of which the humans had not known by which the images could be enlarged. Any part of the transmitted scene could be chosen and examined under high magnification.

Small round men watched those screens, ready to rip off for later study the lasting image should an informative event occur. The images were in full color and of astoundingly fine definition. It was hard to believe that they were transmitted from space by tiny focused tractor and pressor-beams.

The first scenes were wholly peaceful. There was the yellow sun and there were the four planets in plain view. Beyond there were the cold lights of a million million suns of every color and degree of brightness.

As the pseudo-ship rose higher and higher from the cloud-banked globe Rod saw for the first time the actual picturesqueness of interplanetary space. Always, before, when he saw the stars beyond atmosphere, he had had immediate pressing problems of navigation or of survival.

But as a color-picture on a vision-screen its startling beauty and variety struck home. Which proved that Rod was wholly human in failing to notice beauty until a frame was put around it.

Of the enemy ships there was as yet no sign. The drone ship was two thousand miles out. Three. Five. Then warm hands touched Rod and musical notes in his ears formed themselves into words.

The enemy fleet was very close. The crews of its many ships were triumphant by anticipation.

Rod shot the *Stellaris* up to emptiness. For seconds, there seemed to be two Earth-ships in the void. They were identical to all outward appearance and to all seeming they were alone in space.

Suddenly, though, the real *Stellaris* winked out of being. It had gone into the other-space and its only link with the cosmos of the yellow sun was the tenuous complex grid of focused tractor and pressor-beams which linked the drone-ship to the *Stellaris*, the *Stellaris* in turn to two planets of this solar system and to an unthinkably remote unknown object, deep in the heart of the dark universe.

These three anchorages gave the Earthship leverage she needed to maneuver the drone. The television eyes in the drone gave what information was needed to maneuver the drone. The television eyes in the drone gave what information was needed for maneuvers and, of course, the hidden inner weapon began its ceaseless search for targets the instant the *Stellaris* vanished.

The tranquility of airless space remained. The drone-ship — a mere shell — moved like a pawn from another universe, seemed to come to a decision. It swung about in emptiness and headed steadily for the planet of the dead cities.

Its movement was smooth and even, which was in itself a proof that it was not a ship moving on normal drive. A ship under power would either be accelerating or slowing, certainly not coasting at the beginning of an interplanetary voyage.

The dummy space-craft moved on and on. And then something appeared magically, something else appeared magically, suddenly all of space seemed aglitter with shining metal shapes appearing eerily from nowhere.

The yellow sunlight gleamed on their sides, and the vision-screens showed them by myriads in all directions, from a colossal pyramid almost within arm's reach of the drone — it filled all of one television screen — to others and others dwindling through all sizes to the uncertainties of sixth-magnitude brightness.

Within a space of seconds the whole system of the yellow sun was filled with ships. There was no counting them. There were thousands upon thousands upon thousands of them. The pyramid-race had massed such a fleet as Rod had not conceived of to crush the one small vessel which challenged its might and its privilege of assassination.

But the *Stellaris* did represent in fact as great a danger to the murder-race as the pyramid-ships to it. If left undestroyed the *Stellaris* could multiply.

In the dark universe Rod stared in amazement at the spectacle. He touched a single stud, and the drone-ship's weapon lashed out invisibly. But he was almost dazed by the instantaneous appearance of this monstrous fleet.

"They slowed from faster-than-light drive," he said blankly. "That must be it! They traveled in formation, faster than light! And they all slowed together and — here they are! They took my trick of jumping into their laps and twisted it to make their lap jump into me!"

The statement was exact. In the previous fleet-encounter, the *Stellaris* had leaped from extreme range instantly into the midst of the pyramid-ships. There it had done vast damage. Now the enemy fleet had appeared as if leaping from incredible distances, in a formation which could not but surround any space-ship near this sun, with every pyramid-vessel spouting deadly radiation from each of its five flat sides.

Against such a maneuver there could be no defense. It was perfectly designed to wipe out all life in a volume of space exceeding the gravitational field of a sun. Every world and every comet, every asteroid and even every stray grain of meteoric matter — all would be sterilized instantly before a warning-device could operate or a single relay kick over. It was deadliness itself.

And it worked perfectly. The drone-ship was almost crashed by a monster pyramid as it slowed to visibility and ravening beams of push-pull killer-stuff raged through it. That pyramid flung away, keeping formation at many miles a second. Other pyramid-ships flashed past, each one pouring its deadly beams upon the robot vessel. The pseudo-*Stellaris* seemed to falter. Nothing living could survive what it had taken. Nothing could live within it. Nothing!

But the drone-ship fought on. It spun crazily and its beam licked out and licked out and licked out. It bit savagely into the enemy armada as it poured by, every ship flooding the defiant drone with ever-fresh murderousness. Pyramid-ships by dozens and by hundreds hurtled by and each one blasted it afresh.

And each one died. Because whether dead or not, a complicated and inordinately powerful apparatus functioned in the robot, too. Three separate generators — plus a power-supply unit of the enemy's own make — thrust energy eagerly into a push-pull generator which threw a tight aimed beam at every target its detectors disclosed.

That beam far outranged the enemy weapons, because they were practising saturation-beaming and that precluded concentration of their deadliness. So the little robot killed and killed and killed.

But its own lifelessness was certain. Its far-reading murderousness became known but the enemy ships beyond its range exulted in the destruction of the one small crew which was a danger to their race.

Those within range of its weapon, however, were past triumph. They were past everything. They were coffins hurtling onward senselessly.

In other-space, in the *Stellaris'* control-room, warm hands touched Rod. Twitterings became speech. *"More! Kill more of them!"*

Rod said grimly and with narrowed eyes, "I share your ambition. But this is bigger than I expected. They're regrouping now and they must know by this time that the beam that's killing them is working by itself. Every one in range is knocked off and the others are ducking."

Kit said, staring from one to another of the vision-screens, "A terrible lot of them must have been hit, Rod. Look at the way they —"

"There's a terrible lot left," he said bitterly. "We've already knocked off more than were in the entire other fleet, and they know they've been hurt. But look how many are left! I'm worried!"

He sent the drone belligerently at the ships which now drew back from it. But in the space about the yellow sun a curiously dramatic picture formed. The fleet which had already made sure that no life remained on four worlds and the space about them was halting in its plunge.

Scurrying motions took place. Ships whose previous course would have taken them closer to the drone-ship now frantically scurried out of her way but not all of them succeeded.

Yet despite Rod's furious working of controls in other-space there presently developed a regrouping of the untold thousands of angular enemies. The pyramid-ships formed a titanic hollow sphere — and the drone-ship was in its very center.

The drone-ship plunged and spun and plunged again. It succeeded only in violent jerkings and the hollow sphere remained — remained beyond the farthest limit of the robot's range.

In other-space Rod scowled. "They've got pressors on it," he said savagely. "All the whole fleet. Massed pressors — as they massed their killer-beam before. They're holding it still and away from all of them. I haven't got power enough to push-pull it against all that! Looks bad!"

He kept the drone-ship trying frantically to break free but he watched the vision-screens. Time passed. Twitterings sounded behind him, warm hands touched him. The shrill became intelligible.

"They will try to tow it somewhere. Perhaps to their home planet."

"That," said Rod, "I would like to see! But I don't think they will. They build gadgets in their ships to destroy their star-maps when a ship goes dead. They might suspect us of something even more drastic. And if we'd thought of it we would have! I don't know what they'll try but things could look a lot better than they do."

Time passed. Any action among the ships of the hollow globe, of course, was invisible because of the distance. Rod waited grimly, keeping the robot still plunging as if unreasoning mechanism only were at work. But there was something still to be learned.

The pyramid-folk, probably for the first time in their history, had met intelligent and deadly opposition to their career of murder. The opposition had been costly. But they had learned from it. Much too well and much too much! They'd englobed and now held helpless a much more deadly fighting-machine than the *Stellaris* had been only a few days since.

Rod drew in his breath sharply. A little knot of angular ships sped out from the massed armada.

It went swiftly toward the helplessly plunging little ship in the midst of all its enemies.

Warm hands. More twitterings.

"More of them die?"

"Hardly," said Rod angrily. "They learn too quickly! They know nothing can be alive on our ship, though still it fights. So they've set up robot-controls on some of their ships and — we'll see what they do.

"They want to look at the dead crew they think is inside, so they can be sure to massacre the race that bred it. They'd also like to have that fighting-beam, which is better than theirs. And I don't want them to have it!"

Already he had multiplied the deadliness of the alien race by forcing them to devise this new saturation-beaming of a whole solar system. But if each of their ships, in addition, acquired a fighting-beam as deadly as the robot's that would be more serious still.

The moving remotely-controlled pyramid-ships took position on every side of the dummy craft. Its self-directing weapon flooded them with lethal push-pull radiation. It did not affect them. They arranged themselves in a geometric pattern about it. They swayed a little in their respective positions.

Rod, watching through the television eyes, said softly, "Ah-h-h! They've got pressors fanning out! They push against each other but mostly against our double. Now they'll move and take her where they please. But the fleet'll have to cut off its beams!"

He released the directional controls on the locked beams, so the little dummy ship could be moved where the enemy wished. It moved. Its robot escort set out for the nearest planet, which was the world of dead cities.

"They'll ground it," said Rod, "and hold it against the ground and hammer it with another robot ship until they crack it and knock out its beam. Then they'll look it over. *No!*"

Another ship came streaking out of the spherical formation. It had taken longer, perhaps, to fit out with more accurate remote control. It swept in a great curve, matched speed and course with the small convoy, and went along with them for seconds. The dummy Earth-ship seemed to struggle mechanically.

Then there was a sudden flash of light. A thin, concentrated beam of pure flame darted across emptiness. It lanced through the hull of the *Stellaris'* substitute and on beyond for miles. The flame flashed again. Another puncture. A third.

In other-space, a television-screen went dead. There was a sudden crashing noise. A locked beam going from one universe to another went crazy as the object on which it was focused ceased to exist save as blue-white vapor. The robot fighting-ship, helpless now, was being systematically riddled with holes. The process would keep up until its weapon went off and examination by living things became possible.

"We're licked," said Rod coldly. "They're smarter than I thought. They've got us beaten."

He threw over one switch after another. The *Stellaris* surged forward in the dark space where stars were not.

"Rod," asked Kit anxiously. "You mean we can't do anything but run away?"

"Nothing else," he told her. "We simply can't handle that fleet. We can play heck with it — we have — but it's just too big for us. So we depart for new pastures."

Agitated twitterings came from all about him. There was one of the little folk touching Kit for the ability to understand what Rod said. He repeated the confession of defeat. The others made grief-stricken sounds.

"We're still safe ourselves," said Rod over his shoulder. "We're safer probably, than anybody else in the galaxy. And I'm not leaving our dummy for them to paw over. We've just got to start all over again in some new fashion. The only question is, what the heck can the other fashion be?"

He cut off the robot's weapon and watched the television-screens. Suddenly, all the screens went black. There were flute-like wailings from the little folk.

"Tell 'em, Kit," said Rod. "Remember we made our force-fields take in a half-mile sphere of air outside the ship when we wanted to go over that other pyramid? And remember how I sprang the booby-trap before that by tying a string to my coat and pulling it into this space with a focused tractor? And how I sent you a note from the planet when you were in this space?"

"I remember," admitted Kit. "But I don't see —"

"A focused tractor can pull something out of normal space to this, if there's a force-field big enough to hold it. So I pulled our dummy-ship into the dark universe."

There was a resounding crash against the *Stellaris'* hull.

"Here it is," said Rod. "Now we'll get to blazes away from here and figure out what next."

CHAPTER FOURTEEN

New Tactics

FOR hour after hour the *Stellaris* plunged blindly through the utter blackness of other-space with its battered, shat-tered robot-twin in tow. Rod pulled the ship away from the system of the yellow sun by the tractor long ago fixed on an unseen object in darkness' deepest heart.

He could have used the jet-drive but there would have been a trail of vapor — tenuous enough, but possibly followable — when the ejected molecules of gas fell back to normality be-yond the ship's force-fields. Even then the *Stellaris* would be unreachable but there was no point in giving the enemy any clues at all to the nature of its security.

As time went on and acceleration continued the ship reached

the speed of light and multiples of it. Inertia had quite other values here than in the inhabited universe. But whatever they pulled toward was solid and Rod checked its distance by sending pressors to strike it, estimating their time of travel to the strange object.

The small round folk talked interminably among themselves. Joe the electrician, passing by an especially intent conclave, was halted and hands laid upon him. After seconds of listening he sat down absorbedly.

Half an hour later Rod was down in the engine-room working with tractors and pressors that had no wired connections to the control-room. Joe came in search of him.

"Hey!" said Joe. "Those little guys, they got an idea about the way the pyramid-ships go faster than light!"

"Yes?"

"They got it figured out mathematical," said Joe, "that there could be a kinda stuff that ain't natural. That hadn't oughta exist but could get made — or maybe could make itself in a star or something. It wouldn't — uh — react to our magnetism an' it wouldn't be pulled by gravity or anything like that."

"It ought to fall into other-space," objected Rod.

"Only," Joe explained, "it could be alloyed with natural stuff when it got made. And if they had that kinda stuff a little of it would mix with a lot of other stuff and y'could make a ship of it. And that phoney stuff, it would absorb gravity an' magnetism an' so on an' make it damp itself out.

"That's why it wouldn't be pulled by it. But the energy'd have to go somewhere so it'd show up as motion. That's what they say and they say the figures prove it," he added hastily. "It'd be like soaking up heat an' getting electricity. Y'see?"

"Partly," said Rod. Something clicked in a pressor-coil. He looked at the distance-adjustment on the pressor-beam mount. He compared it with a similar guide on a tractor mounting. He began, very delicately, to vary the two together so that neither was subjected to excessive strain.

"So all they'd have to do would be to line up the motion an' they'd have a whale of a drive!" said Joe. "Actually, these guys say that if you got the stuff movin' fast enough it'd start movin' faster on its own account. They say those pyramid-ships could have that stuff in 'em, in all the metal an' such.

"So that all they have to do is pile on their drive-jets until they're goin' fast enough an' they pop into all kindsa speed. It's like runnin' fast enough to catch a train. Once you got holda it, you ain't runnin', you're ridin'.

"Only the train they catch is runnin' all ways at once. Which-ever way they want to go, when they' goin' fast enough all of a sudden they're ridin' 'm an' how! Then all they got to do is slow down when they want to get off."

Rod straightened up and stared. Then he bent over again.

"There's more to it. It has to neutralize increase in mass with velocity and a few little things like that," he observed, "but it does make a certain amount of sense."

"Yeah? But —"

"Ask 'em to figure out two others things," said Rod. "One is how those rats broadcast power, if smashing the generator will cut it off and how fast the cut-off will spread. And the other — I'm asking them to dig into it because I gave them the theory and they've time to work it out and it'll need time and sound thinking — the other is how to make force-fields that will drop matter from this space into ours.

"We can take stuff from our space and drop it into this and hold it here. When we cut out fields it drops back. Now I'm go-ing to want to reverse that process and I think I could do it in time but I'm going quietly mad with stuff that doesn't need that much brains and is even more urgent."

He went back to his pressor and tractor-beams, while Joe returned to the conference of the small people with a puzzled frown on his face.

The ship was crowded but the colonists were civilized and likeable. They crowded themselves to leave room so the humans wouldn't feel crowded. Their women zestfully took over some of the looted fabrics and presently presented Kit with a costume faithfully copying the cut and fit of the one she wore, but breathtaking — in part because of their use of some of the art-objects of unknown origin. The other four girls instantly begged to be similarly attired.

The men conferred and politely asked leave to use an empty store-room for a laboratory. There they conferred endlessly and one of them made computations on an extraordinarily simple machine from the colony and then worked painstakingly with Joe to transfer the equations from his notation to human mathematical terminology.

Rod juggled his beams and juggled them and adjusted them ever more delicately. In the end the *Stellaris* made what might be called a landing on something large and solid in the depths of other-space. Lights thrown out the ports disclosed a rough, seemingly curdled surface of a dark and apparently metallic substance.

Its size was unguessable but it was huge. It had, apparently, no gravitational attraction for the ship — or the drone — and it was plainly not a type of matter normally found in the universe of stars.

When Rod had made tests, he called a conference of all on board. He put his hands on the colony leader so that all could understand him.

"I want to make a report," he told them grimly. "We were licked in our last encounter with the pyramid-ships. But we're vastly better off than we were. Putting extra vegetation in the flotation-bulges has kept our air pure. We've plenty of power and plenty of food. I consider that we can live indefinitely in this ship while we hunt for a planet we can live on.

"We can possibly establish a colony the pyramid-folk will

never find. Certainly we can now build more ships — given materials — which can elude if not defeat those fiends. I don't think it likely that we can ever find our way back to Earth."

A twittering interrupted him. A round little man spoke. Rod understood, but Joe — also touching one of the little folk — translated truculently.

"He says he's been askin' all of us all we knew about the stars we see from Earth. He says he ain't sure, but he thinks there's a chance he can pilot us back to Earth."

There were fifteen humans on the ship. Twelve of them — Rod and Kit and Joe were silent — made a lot of noise. When it ended, Rod went on doggedly. "But back on Earth they didn't believe in danger from the pyramid-people. Whether they'll believe us now or not, I don't know. Certainly it'll take time for them to get ready to fight — if they do.

"But we're ready to fight now. We just got licked, and badly, but we did so much damage that there's a chance the pyramid-people leaders will decide to end their danger immediately by wiping out all races that even promise to achieve civilization. That's what I'm afraid of. If we go on fighting it's going to be bad but —"

He stopped, uncertain what to say next. Joe stood up.

"Anybody that argues," he said belligerently, "is going to get his head knocked off. I seen the dead bodies on that planet."

There was silence. Presently Rod said, "Then I suppose we'll get to work. We're going to make a new weapon and then we're going to find out where those pyramid-people have their home planet. Then we're going to smash it and them. And we'll all probably get gray hair in the process."

There was no discussion. Later the colony leader of the little people came to Rod and touched him and asked earnestly. *"Why did you discuss? Are you not the leader? Why did you explain and why did your friend threaten?"*

"That," said Rod drily, "is what we call democracy."

CHAPTER FIFTEEN

The Rat Trap

THERE was a dark universe unguessable hundreds of millions of light-years in extent. There was a wandering thing in it, a small thing by comparison with the heavenly bodies of star-studded space. In the Earth's solar system it would have been an asteroid, perhaps.

It was barely eight miles through. Its mass could not be measured because it was not a substance which normally existed in normal space. Perhaps it could be created there. Perhaps it was. Possibly it was some unimaginable end-product which remained when the neutronium core of a dwarf star decayed and ceased to be matter that the other universe could retain.

Gravity did not effect it. Magnetism did not draw it. It had no electric conductivity nor did it change the dielectric constant of emptiness. But it was matter of a sort and it could be alloyed with metal.

Rod verified that fact with samples taken in through the air-lock while tractors held the air from flowing out. He gave it to the small folk, saying that it was probably the substance they had deduced from theory could exist.

Their theory suggested other tests, which they made. They went feverishly to work to make alloys. They tore apart the tattered robot-ship with beams which were stronger than the metal they required.

When the alloy was not too high in metal from normal space they found that it was self-welding. Two bits of it, pressed together, united solidly with the strength of a weld.

The small men joyously improvised a process which turned out that alloy as a foil — and the painters on the ship worked at their trade for the first time since leaving Earth. They

114

coated one side of the foil with paint so that it could be stored in rolls without welding itself back to solidity.

Stored it was — placed in storage where no thief or race of thieves imaginable could come upon it. It was piled on the shattered remnant of the drone-ship's plating, anchored to the dark-space object by a tractor with a field of its own to retain it and a generator from the colony to keep it in being.

There were two other generators available. They had been on the drone. There was also the pyramid-ship's power device. The small men had taken that apart and found a surface-treatment of the metal, which to them explained everything. They essayed to give the theory to Rod but he was impatient.

"You say it's a matter of a spherical field practically the diameter of the galaxy, with constants calling for the assumption that space is elastic and can be compressed. All right. It warps so it must be elastic. If it can be compressed the doppler effect on island-universe spectra simply proves distance and not retreat but let it go.

"That's all right — but when you talk about the selective flow of power in a force-field to surface-treated plates because of molecular changes created by the treatment —" Rod shrugged.

"I'll want to know it sometime. The main thing is that the whole field will go off instantly the generator's smashed. I'm not going to try to understand right now. I'm already trying to get some of your math and my head is creaking with the load."

He was trying to check the calculations on a device the colonists were building in their store-room lab. It would, they assured him, create a force-field large enough to shift the entire asteroid into normal space.

The mathematical statements had been translated by Joe and he had — as an electrician working on modern equipment — a mathematical training which once would have implied a master of arts degree. But this math was beyond him and he translated it blindly. Rod was having trouble with it.

In the end he accepted what was not wholly clear because what *was* clear was so evidently right. He wanted to get at the *Stellaris'* force-field generators again. He expanded them to their absolute maximum size. At the new adjustment, the ship would carry a four-mile sphere of normal space into the dark universe when the field went on.

Then he went back to normal space with the ship. She had then been in the dark universe for a long long time and humans and small people alike crowded to the ports to look at the stars. It was strange to see the hunger of both races to look at far-distant suns which now so peculiarly meant home to them.

He'd told Kit his immediate plans and she was ready with half a dozen of the little folk, all solemnly holding hands. The *Stellaris* floated at random amid the stars. Twitterings.

"They say, Rod," reported Kit shakily, "that there aren't any pyramid-people around. Space is empty around here. It's nice, isn't it?"

"Pleasant but not what we need," said Rod. "We'll try again."

The jet-drive went on and the ship went into dark space and came out again light-years away. The little folk solemnly strained for a sense of the emotions of the murderers. Nothing. A second dive and a leap of light-years and a third listening search. A fourth —

Excited twitterings. Hands touched Rod. *"There are many of the murder-race! Many!"*

"Which way?" demanded Rod. "Can you tell? Do they know we're here?"

More flute-like noises.

"They are bored. They know nothing. They are — they are yonder."

A small unhuman hand gestured. Little folk watched avidly as Rod sent a tractor-beam with infinitesimal power groping for the space-ships the small people perceived.

"Got the line," he reported. "Tell me if they're warned."

He swung the *Stellaris*. Jet-drive. A dive and instant emergence from blackness. Nothing. The switches crashed and crashed again. The enemy ships were invisible. Their presence had been detected by the psychic sense of the small people and verified by tractor.

"*Very near,*" said the high-pitched notes. "*Very near! Very, very near. They are frightened! Quick!*"

Rod sent the ship ahead in a desperate leap and the field closed in. The fully-expanded field was like a gigantic net which closed about the Earth-ship.

There was a shrill uproar. The little folk clamored, "*They are frightened. They are helpless! They do not know what has happened!*"

Rod grimly and squeamishly changed the controls on the *Stellaris'* bow-weapon.

"I never could kill a rat in a trap," he said savagely. "Here! *You* do it!"

He put the warm, non-human hand of the leader of the little round colonists upon a switch.

"Throw it — and they'll die."

There was a tumult of shill voices. The *Stellaris* had winked out of other-space and instantly vanished into it again. But with her in her vanishing had gone the contents of a four-mile sphere of emptiness. As once she had carried air to the dark universe, now she carried — nothing, on the first attempts.

But this time the force-field had enclosed a pyramid-ship inside it with the *Stellaris*. Once before such a vessel had been dragged into the illimitable dark but the crew of that one had been dead. The crew of this was yet alive.

The little folk shrilled at one another in a terrible joy. Their leader trembled with his satisfaction as he savagely threw the switch which sent a beam of utter deadliness into the captive enemy.

It was a trivial payment for the millions upon millions of their fellows but the small people were filled with impassioned joy. They felt — they *felt!* — the murderers of their race blasted out of life.

"The answer," said Rod, seeing Kit's expression, "is that their power-supply only works in normal space. We ought to know that. So when I snatched them out of the natural universe into this one their power went, their weapons were useless and I think that even the gadget that destroys their star-maps failed to work. At least, that's what I'm after!"

He went to the air-lock, in which were mounted tractor and pressor-beams and a powerful mounted light. With tractors the enemy ship was brought alongside the *Stellaris*. The two air-locks were lined up.

And — this was the ticklish part — while tractors again kept air from escaping Rod and a welder cut through into the pyramid-ship and went into the revolting reek which was its atmosphere.

With hand-flashes Rod and those who would help him made their way to where only molten metal and charred paper had remained on the other ship they'd searched. But here — here were shining unfamiliar instruments and infinitely ingenious star-maps and all that could be needed to navigate a pyramid-ship the length and breadth of the galaxy.

Rod had Joe and two others load themselves down. He himself carried precious maps. They returned to the *Stellaris*. A dozen of the small men followed them back to the ship from the blasted enemy, but it was significant that not one of the round men carried a single object as a trophy. Their hatred of the killers of their race was too great to let them look at even a memento without rage.

The *Stellaris* headed back through dark-space for the asteroid of dark-space matter. Rod and the colony mathematicians
pored over the maps and astrogation instruments. But they
knew the principles by which such things must work and the
secrets came easily.

By the time they were near the asteroid the matter was
settled. Rod returned to normal space and checked his observations. The colony power-technician by then had worked out
a field-flow instrument to detect the power-field of the enemy
and to locate its center. His observation checked with the
star-maps. Everything checked.

The ship was filled with fluting sounds. The round small
colonists were strangely moved. They knew that their dead
cities, their dead world, their dead race would soon be avenged.
But Rod, touching hands for technical reasons, heard distressed
discussions in the back-ground.

The small people had craved vengeance with a fierceness
close to insanity, as long as they had little hope of it. But now
they had savored it. They had known fully the helpless,
screaming panic of the crew which had had to be killed.

It could not be spared.

Descriptions of either of the two races in the *Stellaris* could
not be allowed to go back to the leaders of the pyramid-folk.
So the pyramid-ship's crew had to die. But a discussion went
on in the Earth-ship with mounting distress.

To destroy a race because it had destroyed one's own might
be just and proper — but it made one a murderer too.

And the small people were an inherently gentle folk.

The preparations for moving the dark asteroid to normal
space were almost complete when something like a deputation
of the colonists came to Rod. The round men were very unhappy, but very much in earnest. Rod touched hands and the
shrill sounds about him were somehow very solemn.

"We ask," said the leader unhappily, "that we be taken to

a near planet we find on the alien's star-maps. As we read the
maps, we should be able to live there. We owe you our lives
and any hope our race can have of surviving through us and
our children.

"If you ask it, we will remain and help you even to the de-
struction of the murderers of our kin. But unless you ask we
prefer to try to build up a new civilization without protection.
We have tasted revenge — and we do not like it."

Rod regarded them steadily. "I don't like killing, either," he
said grimly. "I weakened just now. I gave the task to one of
you. But I am wondering now if a fleet may not be going
through one solar system after another, wiping out the life to
be found there.

"I am wondering if such a fleet has reached my home planet
yet. I am wondering if the fifteen of us humans on this ship
are the only human beings still alive — as you are the only
living members of your race. I don't want to leave my race in
danger for one instant if it's living.

"And if it's dead," he added harshly, "I want it to be avenged
before I find out! I don't want to keep on living while I hate
creatures I have spared. But I'll take you to the planet you've
chosen. We need some fresh observations anyhow."

CHAPTER SIXTEEN

Nova!

EVERYTHING was quite ready when the *Stellaris* went a
bare thousand miles from the strange thing it had made
of an asteroid, and returned to normal space. Then, with
the jet-drive to set its course and establish a velocity, it dived
back to darkness to increase that velocity, and came out yet
again into the space where suns flamed grandly, surrounded

by their families of planets. They were near their destination.

This also was a sol-type sun and it had seven planets. The nearest was red-hot from its proximity to its sun. The second was an arid waste, the third a small and pock-harked cinder. But the fourth was green, with great oceans and clouds floating above its continents and ice-caps at its poles.

"*There is a race here,*" said apologetic twitterings in Rod's ear. "*It is still barbarous, knowing metals but using no power, according to the markings we diciphered on the star-map. It will be long before it should cause the pyramid-people concern. Perhaps we may help and guide the people.*"

Rod said nothing. He made a planetary approach with something approaching professional skill. In hardly more than minutes the *Stellaris* settled down into atmosphere.

"Rod!" cried Kit. "A city!"

She pointed and Rod swung the ship — so unwieldy in air — into a near approach. It reached the city. It hovered over the city. It was a city, past question. Its ways were paved with quarried stone, its buildings were of massive, cyclopean architecture and it was barbarously magnificent.

But it was definitely barbarous. The great buildings were palaces and temples. The people lived in small structures, most of which plainly had gardens attached to them. There were cultivated fields and pasture-lands outside it. There were crude wooden ships tied to the wharves where a river wandered through it.

As the *Stellaris* descended Rod saw half-furled sails. Sails had not been used on Earth except for sport in two hundred years. But he saw no movement.

There was no movement.

The *Stellaris* touched ground. Very grim indeed, Rod led the way to the airlock. He opened it.

There was a smell in the air. It was the smell of death.

"These people were hardly more than savages," said Rod

very quietly, "and they were alive no more than two or three days ago. They haven't even motors! By what we can see they must have lighted their homes with flames, burning the fat of animals, or petroleum.

"They had no fliers, no ground-vehicles except —" he pointed — "that was a vehicle, with an animal pulling it. And these people were killed because some day they might have made a space-ship. The pyramid-folk are frightened. *We've* frightened them.

"They're wiping out all intelligent life that can challenge them even a thousand years from now! If you want to spare yourselves the grief of killing these fiends, go ahead! Get out! Quickly! *I've* got work to do!"

But none of the small people moved to land.

Their leader touched hands with Rod.

"We have decided again," his shrill notes said. *"We fight. Not to avenge our dead but to protect those who will never know that we lived. Please! Make haste!"*

The *Stellaris* rocketed skyward and went into blackness, then sped madly to the dark asteroid with her jet-drive and tractors together striving for the utmost speed.

In an hour the force-fields were shrunk so that only the *Stellaris* was included in them. But before that time and under their shielding, the foil-rolls were unrolled. As they touched the dark mass they were welded inseparably to its surface. The other devices needed also were welded fast and the *Stellaris* anchored herself solidly with tractors, and a pressor irrevocably thrust home the master-switch.

Instantly from the ports of the ship — from which glaring lights had shone — there was only the blackness of empty dark-space. The asteroid had vanished. But the *Stellaris* remained anchored to it and the *Stellaris* stayed in dark-space. The ship was with its creation but in dimensions parallel to those of the universe of stars. There was reason.

There were three vision-plates in the ship's control-room, which reported from the asteroid as they had reported from the drone. Starlight shone on the metal of the ungainly object's surface for the first time since time began.

The report the vision-eyes sent to the dark universe was beyond all expectations and beyond the experience of any save members of the race which made shining ships and used them for unwarned murder. It was terrifying. And it was sublime.

The asteroid reached normal space with a velocity which was inherent — and which was above the critical speed of the alloy-plates now welded to it. Those plates bit hard into the substance of the new universe. They were of the stuff which sent pyramids at deadly multiples of the speed of light.

Other-space matter and normal-space matter, alloyed together, were an unholy compound which consumed the energy of gravitation and of magnetism and of the energy which is electrostatic stress. Perhaps it even consumed the energy of light. And all of that energy it transformed into motion, having a velocity in miles-per-second to begin with.

It sped at a mounting speed which turned all visible starlight to violet, then turned all heat-rays to blue. And still its rate of progress grew. It sped faster until light itself had no meaning and radio-frequency radiations were light and then even they were nothing.

It hurtled onward and the television-screens saw all the universe in that unimaginable glow which is the slow pulsation of the hearts of suns, taking hours to the beat, but now raised in frequency to a strange and eerie glow. And still the speed increased.

Rod worked controls, his eyes shining like coals. There would be but one chance to use this weapon, this bolt of other-matter from another space, traveling at a rate beside which light-speed was imperceptible. The accuracy of the shot must be absolute. There must be no deviation of the thousands of a hair. And the time was very, very short.

Actually, the thing happened in seconds.

The sun the aliens' star-maps pictured lay ahead. It was a giant sun, so huge and fierce that the aliens' inhabited planet lay two-hundred-million miles away. It was toward that sun that the other-space projectile sped. It was miles in diameter, but it could be controlled.

It moved at five thousand times the speed of light but Rod had precious moments in which to observe its course and aim it, seconds in which to adjust the aim, fractions of seconds in which to make sure.

Then he cut loose the anchoring tractors and the *Stellaris* floated on while the hurtling thing went unguided.

The Earth-ship returned to normal space far beyond the solar system of the pyramid-makers. And the thing was already finished. But the light had not yet reached this spot.

Those on the Earth-ship had time to line the ports, staring, and see the giant sun and even to glimpse the shining specks which were its worlds before the spectacle began.

They did not see the missile strike. No eyes could follow the mass which struck at thousands of millions of miles per second, with all the stored energy in its impact that it had absorbed from the linkage-fields across its path. They could not even tell where it had struck.

They saw only that the great sun swelled suddenly and swelled again with a monstrous and terrible deliberation, then seemed to pour out into all space as if to devour it utterly. The timing was like the seemingly slow-motion process of water falling over Victoria Nyanza falls.

Actually it was of incredible vehemence and unthinkable force. The free energy within the sun had suddenly been tripled by the arrival of that supernal missile, which sank to the sun's very heart before its atoms could explode.

The sun literally detonated. Flaming ravening star-stuff shot outward at thousands of miles-per-second. A planet was engulfed — a second. A third, fourth, fifth and sixth.

Those on the *Stellaris* watched the sun become a nebula, a mass of incandescent gas filling a globe five-thousand-million miles across. And no planet lived in that inferno — no gigantic generator of power, able to supply thousands of murder-fleets light-millennia away, could still be functioning. The planet of the pyramid-ships was gone. Its sun had blown itself to vapor.

And no pyramid-ship anywhere in the galaxy had power.

Those in motion past the speed of light stayed in motion. There was no power in them to brake below the critical speed of the alloy of which they were made. Those below the speed of light had no power to rise to it. Those in planetary atmospheres fell heavily in the ground. Those grounded stayed aground.

But most of the murder-fleets out upon the errand of wholesale massacre so lately commanded and not yet completed — most of them drifted on unendingly. A few suns acquired small fleets of pyramidal satellites. One or two planets captured brightly-polished moons.

And of course there were some meteoric falls, which, when excavated, disclosed half-fused artifacts and dead aliens with bulbous heads and attenuated arms and legs. But most of the pyramid-ships simply drifted on — and on — and on.

Forever.

* * * * *

When the *Stellaris* got back to her own solar system it was necessary to be very careful. Not because of fear from any Earth-defense but lest she do damage. The bow-weapon had to be turned off completely. Tractor and pressor scanning-beams could not be used, of course, when nearing a planet with so precariously poised a civilization as Earth's.

And then it was distinctly quaint that as she lowered heavily into atmosphere Earth-Government planes darted upon her, firing furiously, and had to be pushed away with pressors as the ship went tiredly to ground.

Then there were investigations and vast excitement and much indignation. Rod Cantrell, said solemn individuals in Earth Government, had departed from Earth without authorization in the only vessel capable of space-navigation and defense of the human race against certain strange alien spaceships which had plunged to their destruction upon the Earth's surface.

Who knew, said these indignant people, how many more alien ships were floating about outside the Earth's atmosphere, preparing for invasion and the capture of Sol's fairest planet?

Rod said curtly that there were no more alien ships about. Glowering a little, he made his report. Those who had been of the unwilling crew of the *Stellaris* substantiated it. The small round people of the planet of dead cities told in their fluting voices what had become of their race. Earth Government gave them a space-ship, ultimately, and they went back to build up their civilization anew.

In the end the court-martial at which this testimony came out was ended and Rod Cantrell was formally absolved of all penalty for having been on board the *Stellaris* when a short-circuit threw it into space.

He was cleared of all censure for having saved the ship and those in it and no blame — so the verdict ran — lay upon him for having fought the murderers of a thousand civilizations and for having certainly prevented the ending of humanity.

And then, as a separate and necessarily slow process, there began the tedious, red-tape-filled process of rewarding him. In the course of a year or so he would undoubtedly be given a medal.

But he was not concerned. A month after the *Stellaris'* return to Earth there were fluting sounds in the anteroom of the quarters he occupied. The leader of the colonists from the planet of dead cities wished to confer with him. Rod liked the little round man but he begged off.

Kit said, "Why'd you do that, Rod? He's a nice little person."

"I know," said Rod. "But d'you remember how little attention I paid to you while we were off in the *Stellaris?*"

"I certainly do!" said Kit.

"I was busy," Rod explained amiably. "But I just got leave for our marriage and a honeymoon. And I thought that since I neglected you so much before — well — I thought I'd put everything else aside and pay a little attention to you now."

THE END

www.ingramcontent.com/pod-product-compliance
Lightning Source LLC
Chambersburg PA
CBHW050801250626
47155CB00005B/2161